MASTER CROOK'S CRIME ACADEMY

BURGLARY FOR BEGINNERS

Look out for more escapades

MASTER CROOK'S CRIME ACADEMY

ROBBERY FOR RASCALS

CLASSES IN KIDNAPPING

MASTER CROOK'S CRIME ACADEMY

BURGLARY FOR BEGINNERS

A BOOK THIS FUNNY
SHOULD BE
AGAINST THE LAW!

From the creator of
HORRIBLE HISTORIES™

TERRY DEARY

Illustrated by John Kelly

■ SCHOLASTIC

For Lisa Edwards

First published in the UK in 2009 by Scholastic Children's Books
An imprint of Scholastic Ltd
Euston House, 24 Eversholt Street
London, NW1 1DB, UK
Registered office: Westfield Road, Southam, Warwickshire, CV47 0RA
SCHOLASTIC and associated logos are trademarks and/or registered
trademarks of Scholastic Inc.

ISBN 978 1 407 11015 8

Printed and bound in the UK by CPI Mackays, Chatham, ME5 5TD
Papers used by Scholastic Children's Books are made from wood grown in
sustainable forests.

1 3 5 7 9 10 8 6 4 2

This is a work of fiction. Names, characters, places, incidents and dialogues are
products of the author's imagination or are used fictitiously. Any resemblance to
actual people, living or dead, events or locales is entirely coincidental.

www.scholastic.co.uk/zone

CONTENTS

Before word

You may not remember 1837. You are probably a bit too young. You may be one of those sad people who have been forced to go to school – a punishment far worse than five years in Darlham Gaol if you ask me! But, if you have been to school, your history teacher may have told you that 1837 was the year the old queen came to the throne.

It was quite a large throne because she had a large bottom, of course. In fact she was a short but wide young lady at the time. She grew wider as years passed. Several people tried to shoot her, as you know. They all missed. How they missed such a w-i-d-e target I'll never know.

Those are the sorts of things the history books will tell you. But the story I have to tell you is not so well known. That's because it all happened in a quaint, coastal town in a northern corner of the country. What happened there was sensational. Sensational. If it had happened in the capital of our country then the history books would be full of it.

But it didn't. It happened in the poor little, muddy

little, cold little, wind-wracked, wave-washed, smoke-choked, rat-riddled, sour-smelling little town of Wildpool. A town that time forgot. A midden that's hidden.

I like that phrase, don't you? Of course you youngsters may not know what a midden is. In these days of dustcarts and flushing toilets no one has a midden any more. It was a rubbish tip made up of ashes and all the disgusting things that nobody wanted. Just like Wildpool in fact.

So the story is almost forgotten. You can find parts of this tale in the pages of old newspapers, a few faded diaries and town council reports, the odd letter and scraps of dusty paper.

It would take a long time for you to gather the pieces and make sense of the story, so I have done it for you. I have spent a lifetime gathering the facts and the papers so I can share the story with you.

It is the story of a great plague of crime that swept over Wildpool like one of the winter waves on Wildpool beach sweeps over the pier. A crime wave!

Another little phrase I have invented and that I like a lot. I think it could catch on. But I am interrupting. "Again!" you cry. Sorry. I will try to control myself. Forgive me if I burst out into twittering notes like a skylark. It is the excitement, you know.

And 1837 was an odd time to see such a surge of crime. Your history teacher will have told you that in the 1830s the famous Robert Peel invented the police force to stamp out crime in the country.

So, why (you ask) did crime in Wildpool get worse, not better when the first police began to patrol?

I will tell you, I reply. That is what my story aims to do.

Who am I? and why am I so interested in the Wildpool wave of crime? You ask (you do ask a lot of questions, don't you?).

I will not tell you who I am. All I will say is this: I saw what happened because I was there at the time. I may appear in the pages of this superior story . . . but you will not know it is me.

Why? You ask. Why do I wish to stay hidden in my own tale? Well, some of the things I did were outside the law. I am not ashamed of what I did. But I am too old to go to jail for crimes that happened over sixty years ago.

Read on for a chronicle of crime that will chill you colder than the East wind that whistled through the Wildpool streets that winter.

A tale of terror, of treasure and of Twistle.

Mr X

22 January 1901

No, Mr X is not my real name. In fact I may not even be a Mr. Perhaps I am a Miss or a Mrs, a Lady or a Lord! But I promised to stop cutting in with these needless notes, didn't I? So don't read this one.

Chapter 1

GRAVE WORDS
OF GRANNY

"Never forget," Mrs Smith said. "Never forget what
your granny said with her last breath."

"What was that, Mum?" a boy with ragged black
hair breathed.

"Your granny looked up from her deathbed—"

"I thought she was run over by a muck cart," the
boy interrupted.

"She was, Smiff."

*Yes, that is right. The boy was called Smiff
Smith. His mother had to register his name in the
church when he was born. When the clerk*

asked the boy's name she said, "Smith" . . . as you would! The clerk wrote it down as his FIRST name AND managed to spell it wrong . . . he didn't want to cross it out or change it because he felt a bit of a prawn. So Smiff Smith was given his name.

Birth Registration 1827

Name: Smiff Smith,
Father: Silas Smith, occupation "Sea Captain (deceased)"
Mother: Belinda Smith, occupation "Coal worker"
Place of birth: 71 Low Street, Wildpool.

The woman went damp around the eyes. "We carried her into the house and laid her on the kitchen table," Mrs Smith said and sniffed sadly.

"So it wasn't a death bed?"

Mrs Smith was starting to look a bit cross and her lips went thin and white. "All right. Your granny looked up from her death table and said, 'Never forget, Belinda . . . You can never have too many mop buckets!' "

"Too many mop buckets? What's that supposed to mean?" the boy asked.

Mrs Smith shrugged. "Dunno, Smiff. She died before she could tell us. Oh, how I cried!"

"Because Granny was dead?" He asked gently.

"No, because we couldn't afford a funeral!" she snapped.

"What did you do?"

Mrs Smith shrugged. "It was the muck cart that ran her down, remember, so it was the muck cart that carried her away to the town dump. She didn't mind. She was dead."

Smiff peered at his mum through the sputtering light of the mutton-fat candle.

"Are you lying, Mum?"

She smiled her twisted smile. "All our family tell lies, Smiff. It's what we do best. You know that. But I've never forgotten your granny's last words and I've never been short of mop buckets. Go out and get me one, son."

Smiff sighed. The coal fire was glowing warm. The street cobbles outside were covered in ice and he had no shoes to his name.

That's an odd thing to say. No shoes to his "name". Why don't people say, "I had no shoes to my feet"? Or "No shoes to my shoe-cupboard"? I don't know. I thought you might know. Excuse me for asking.

Smiff was thin as a rat's tail and had no fat to keep out the cold from his bones.

"Aw, Mum!" he groaned.

Mrs Smith grabbed him by the collar and hissed at him through her yellow teeth. "You wouldn't refuse a dying granny's last wish, would you?"

"No, Mum," he sighed. The boy wrapped a blanket around his shoulders, took one last loving look at the fire and pushed the door open.

The wind was sharper than a butcher's knife, slicing through his blanket and thin shirt. "Why doesn't Mum ever send me out to steal something useful," he muttered through his chattering teeth.

 *The teeth were chattering to each other as there was no one else in the street to chatter to. But at least they had each other. It is very lonely having no one to chatter to. Granny had a lonely tooth before she died. A single tooth in the middle of her mouth. She was the first woman in the country to have central eating.*

"Something like a warm, woollen coat?" But she never did.

He stepped over the horse droppings and crossed

the road by the green-glowing gas lamp. The wind stabbed at him as he climbed up the steep hill of Low Street. At the top he turned towards the High Street. He hurried past dark alleys. A clumsy dust-cart driver almost ran him down . . . Smiff thought the man may have been trying to. "Mum would send me to my funeral on your cart!" he shouted at the man but the clattering hooves and rattling of wheels on the cold cobbles drowned his voice.

At last he reached the row of shops. The apothecary with glowing glass globes of red, blue and yellow liquid cast their rainbow light on the pavement. Smiff hurried past. The wizened wizard who owned the shop was as scary as a rat with rabies and twice as ugly.

He trotted on past the grocer, the greengrocer and the baker, the hat shop and the pawnbroker till he reached the hardware shop with its tin pots and clothes pegs, china cups and pewter mugs. Smiff slipped through a maze of ropes and riddles, candles and cart-grease, buckets and brooms, knives and forks, hammers and handsaws.

The boy picked up a hammer. He picked up a mop

bucket. He looked around. He felt something was watching him. There was no one there . . . or so he thought.

He smashed the hammer against the side of the mop bucket then marched up to the counter.

A thin old man stood there, as grey as the boy's blanket, and peered at him. "My mother is mad," Smiff said.

"Then see a doctor," the old man told him in his creaking-floorboard voice.

"I mean angry-mad. You sold her this bucket and it has a dent in the side!" Smiff showed him the dent he had just made. "She wants a new one, or else!"

"Else?"

"Else she'll come down here with her wet mop and shove it up your nose . . . she says!"

"Better take a new one, son," the shop owner sighed. "I'll lose the money it cost me," he said, shaking his head.

Smiff almost felt sorry for him. But when the old man stepped from behind the counter the boy saw he was wearing boots. He must be rich, Smiff decided.

The boy left the shop with a shining new mop

bucket wrapped in brown paper.

A man in a shabby top hat stood on the street corner. His gooseberry-green eyes glowed in the gas-light. His fingers were fine as twigs on a vine. They rippled when he talked.

As Smiff walked past him he clapped his hands softly. "Well done, my little thief," he said. "You almost got away with that."

The boy shivered and it wasn't with the cold. "Are you a watchman?" he asked.

The man smiled and ivory teeth glowed under his thick, dark moustache. "No. Not the watch. I am Samuel Dreep, a teacher."

"I've heard about teachers," Smiff shuddered. "They take rich children into schools and beat them till they learn."

"I don't work for that sort of school," Dreep laughed. "I will walk with you back to your house in Low Street and explain. . ."

"You know where I live?"

"Oh, yes, young Smiff. We know a lot about you. You are the sort of young man who will do very well in our new school."

12

"But Mum taught me how to read and do letters," Smiff boasted.

"Ah, no," Dreep said shaking his head. The two walked down Low Street and the man trod carefully so his leather boots didn't slip on the icy cobbles. "I am a teacher at the famous Master Crook's Crime Academy and I believe I can help you. Come with me."

"Master Crook's Crime Academy? I've never heard of it."

"It's secret . . . but the name is famous in certain parts of the city. Let me show you."

He pulled out a neat piece of cardboard with a printed picture of a fine house. The boy held it under the light of a flaring gas lamp to read it.

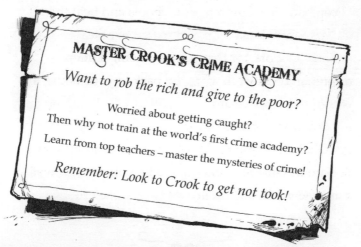

MASTER CROOK'S CRIME ACADEMY

Want to rob the rich and give to the poor?

Worried about getting caught?
Then why not train at the world's first crime academy?
Learn from top teachers – master the mysteries of crime!

Remember: Look to Crook to get not took!

"Get not took?" Smiff blinked.

"Get not caught . . . don't get caught," Dreep shrugged. "But 'get not took' sounds better. It's poetry."

Smiff shook his head.

"My mum needs her mop bucket," he said and hurried on.

"She has enough mop buckets," the tall man cried.

"You can never have too many mop buckets," Smiff said. "Never!"

He led the way through the battered front door into the dark hallway of his house. It smelled of dead cats and cabbage. "Hi, Mum! We have a visitor," he said and hurried into the warmth of the living room that smelled of dead cabbage and cats. "This is Mr Samuel Dreep."

Mrs Smith looked up and patted her bird's nest of hair. "Ooooh! Mr Dreep, sir, you caught me all unprepared. Smiff shouldn't go bringing gentlemen in without warning. I mean . . . with my make-up on and my best dress I look ten years younger. Ooooh, I don't know where to put myself."

Samuel Dreep stepped forward and took Mrs Smith's hand. He raised it to his lips and kissed the grubby paw.

"Mrs Smith, you already look ten years younger."

"Ten years younger than what?"

"Ten years younger than Granny," Smiff muttered.

"Your son is so talented," Dreep went on. "A thief as skilful as a cat in a cream factory."

"He is that," Mrs Smith beamed. "Taught him myself."

"I am here to make you an offer. Send him to Master Crook's Crime Academy and he will make you a nice little income for your old age."

"Old age?" she said sharply.

"And your young age! We will train your son in the art of crime. No more stealing trifles like mop buckets. He will bring you diamonds to sparkle like your bright eyes, gold to fill your shining silk purse and dresses of satin to show off your fine figure!"

"Ooooh! Mr Dreep," she giggled like a girl being tickled in a feather factory. "You are naughty." She turned to her son. "Here, Smiff, fill the mop bucket from the pump in the yard and boil some water over the fire. I'm sure Mr Dreep would like a cup of tea. "

"Aw, Mum! I just got warm again."

"No tea for me," Dreep put in quickly.

Can you blame him? I mean, Mr Dreep liked tea — we all do. But to know it was boiled in a mop bucket is not a nice thought. Mop buckets are very useful . . . as we shall see . . . and you can never have too many. But please don't use them to make tea.

"I am from Master Crook's Crime Academy and I want to invite young Smiff to join. I can make him a master of the art of crime. The school opens its doors for the first time tomorrow. Your son can be one of the first pupils. He can make it to the very top."

Dreep pulled a square of paper from inside his coat and slipped it on to the table in front of Mrs Smith. Smiff looked at it. Mrs Smith looked at it.

"We call it a school-home contract," Dreep explained.

"Ooooh! There now, Smiff!" she sighed.

MASTER CROOK'S CRIME ACADEMY

I Belinda Smith hereby agree to enrol my son Smiff Smith in the school known as Master Crook's Crime Academy.

I also swear on my granny's teeth:

- not to tell anyone about my child's school or snitch to the law
- to make sure s/he sticks to the school rules at all times and doesn't skive or play truant
- to make sure s/he does their homework
- to support the teachers even if they give him/her a smack round the ear for being cheeky
- to make sure he has the school uniform and a good pair of boots.

The school agrees to:

- give you half of what your child makes from his/her crimes
- pay for your child's funeral if s/he has an accident while doing a dangerous job OR gets caught and is hanged.

Signed

Belinda Smith

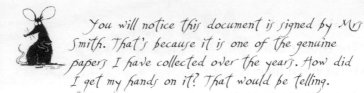

You will notice this document is signed by Mrs Smith. That's because it is one of the genuine papers I have collected over the years. How did I get my hands on it? That would be telling.

Mrs Smith laughed, "That looks very fair to me. Very fair."

"I don't like that bit about being caught and hanged, Mum," Smiff frowned.

"It's all right, son!" She grinned her yellow-toothed grin. "The school will pay. I know you are worried about your dear mum having to fork out for a funeral. No need. Look. It's here on the paper." She ruffled his black hair playfully.

"No, Mum, paying for my funeral isn't what I was worried about," Smiff said angrily.

"Look, son, what are the chances of you being caught? Eh? The town watch are a bunch of old men that have more noses between them than teeth. They couldn't catch a dead dog if it ran into the town jail and gave itself up."

"Now then, Mrs Smith," Samuel Dreep said softly. "I think there is one small matter I have to tell you about. It's only fair."

"Small matter?"

"The small matter of the town watchmen."

"What about them?"

"They won't be around for much longer," Dreep said and stroked his moustache carefully.

"All the better for Smiff!" Mum shrugged.

"No. What I mean is they are about to be replaced. There is a new sort of law officer about to walk the streets of Wildpool."

"Ooooh! Hear that, Smiff? A new sort of law officer about to walk the streets of Wildpool," his mother said and poked him in the shoulder.

"Yes, Mum, I'm not deaf. I suppose these new officers will be sharper than the old watchmen, will they?" Smiff groaned. "I suppose there'll be more chance of me dangling on the end of a hangman's rope?"

"It depends who gets the officers' jobs," Dreep said with a soft smile.

"I still don't like the sound of these new officers. What are they called?"

"They are called police," the tall man said.

"Sound horrible." The boy sighed. "Don't sign that paper yet, Mum."

Mrs Smith waved it happily in the candlelight. "Too late, son, too late. It's all done. You start at Master Crook's Crime Academy tomorrow."

"Thanks, Mum," Smiff said bitterly. "Thanks."

"That's all right, son," the woman said and wrapped an arm around his thin shoulders. "Master Crook will make sure those nasty Please Men don't get you. Isn't that right, Mr Dreep?"

"We're working on it right now," Dreep said. "Right now. . ."

Chapter 2

TRUNCHEONS OF FIRE

Wildpool town hall was the pride of the town and Wildpool's mayor was the pride of . . . well, the pride of himself.

Tall and handsome, elegant and awesome . . . I mean the town hall, of course, not the mayor. Smoke stained and with twiddly knobs struck on . . . I mean the town hall, not the mayor. A neat little beard, a pair of gold-rimmed spectacles and a fine black suit . . . I mean the mayor, not the town hall.

The mayor was Sir Oswald Twistle. A legend in his own mind. A man as tall as any gnome, as mean as a wasp with toothache and as rich as a conquering king.

He had the mighty brain of a turnip . . . as large as a turnip but not quite so clever.

Sir Oswald said his family arrived with William the Conqueror back in 1066. Sadly they decided to stay.

He used his wealth to bribe and buy people and of course they made him mayor. It was worth every golden coin to Twistle to stand there on the town-hall stage and speak to his adoring people in front of his adoring wife.

"People of Wildpool!" he cried. There were at least twelve people crowding into the council chamber that was big enough to hold a hundred. "People of Wildpool!" he repeated. His voice was a little squeaky and didn't sound quite so grand as he imagined. Mayor Twistle turned to his wife who sat on a velvet chair behind him. "I just said 'people of Wildpool' twice, dear," he muttered.

His wife, Arabella Twistle, had written the speech for him. She always wrote his speeches. She was a large woman. She was a very large woman. Her dress of pale green silk would have made a fine sail for one of the ships in Wildpool harbour. Her face would have made an even finer figurehead on the bow.

The Twistles

You know what a figurehead is, don't you? One of those wooden women who were stuck to the front of sailing ships back in those days. They stared ahead and dared the seas to do their worst. Arabella Twistle's wooden face would not have dared the seas . . . it would have scared the seas. Waves would have run and hidden under the nearest island.

"Yes, Ossie, dear. You have to say it twice to grab your listeners by the ear. Make them sit up and listen!"

"They are standing up," the mayor said.

Under the hard white mask of make-up, Arabella Twistle's face began to glow as pink as the lace bonnet that framed her fat face. A face as hard as the diamonds that lay on her large, white chest. "Read it, Oswald. Read it. Trust me. I am the best writer in Wildpool – probably the best writer in the whole country. Read it!"

The mayor gave a single nod and turned back to the crowd of eleven . . . one had slipped out to the toilet. "People of Wildpool!" he cried.

"You already said that," a blind beggar sniffed. He was only in there to get out of the cold.

"People of Wildpool!" the mayor repeated.

"Four times," the beggar sighed.

"Today is a day that will go down in the annals of Wildpool history!" Mayor Twistle read.

"What's annals?" someone cut in.

Lady Arabella leaned forward and spat, "Books. History books."

"Right!"

"This very day the streets of Wildpool will be safe for all decent people to walk abroad. To tread the precious cobbles of our glorious town, knowing that we are safe from the dangers of thieves, rogues, varlets and beggars."

"You what?" said the beggar.

Twistle read on. "People of Wildpool! I, Oswald Twistle, your mayor, am proud and honoured to announce that we will have a new force of law and order walking the streets. A police force!"

"What's that then?" one of the twelve asked. (Yes, the twelfth one was back from the toilet.)

"Men in uniform will patrol the streets and guard our persons, guard our homes, guard our factories and guard our wealth!"

25

"I haven't got any wealth," the blind beggar snapped.

Sir Oswald Twistle ignored him. "A new law allows us to have one police officer for every thousand people in the town. Wildpool has two thousand people. So we will be guarded not by one lone police officer, but by two . . . or three if we count the inspector in charge."

Arabella Twistle leaned forward to explain. "Though of course the inspector will not be walking the streets. He will be at the station."

"Waiting for a train?" the beggar asked.

"The police station, not the railway station," Lady Twistle hissed. "A new building at the side of the town jail. Very handy for locking up people like you . . . so watch it, mate."

"Here don't you go threatening me!" the beggar croaked. "I've not done nothing wrong!"

"My police will find something if you don't shut your ugly mouth," her ladyship spat.

"Ugly? That's the cat calling the pottle black. You're as ugly as—"

"Stop!" Mayor Twistle shouted. "Stop it. Let me finish my speech." Silence fell over the mighty crowd. The mayor shook his paper and read. "I will sweep the

streets of Wildpool clean of the filth that fouls its gutters. I will give us a town to be proud of. A town . . . wipe a tear from your eye . . . eh?" He looked back at his wife.

"No-o!" she moaned. "You do that . . . wipe a tear away . . . you don't say it!"

"Sorry, dear." He turned to face his public. "A town . . . sniffle . . . where our children can play happily in the parks of green. . ."

"They'll have to watch out for the dogs' droppings," a mother muttered.

"Where we can walk safely in the streets. . ."

"Not to mention the horse droppings," her friend added.

"Tonight it is my great honour, joy and delight to introduce to you . . . the men who will guard us like the angels that they are!" Mayor Twistle waved a little hand to the door at the side of the chamber.

The door creaked open a crack. "Now?" a voice whispered.

Twistle nodded. "Constable Liddle and Constable Larch!"

The old oak door was flung open and two men stepped out shyly. They blinked in the bright gaslight that flooded over the stage. Constable Liddle was as

old as the oak that made the door and thinner than one of its twigs. His wispy white moustache trailed like a sad dog's tail.

"He looks just like the old watchman but dressed in a new uniform," the woman whispered to her neighbour.

"That's cos he is the old watchman dressed in a new uniform," her friend replied.

"Oh, good! I thought me eyes were playing tricks!"

Liddle shuffled along and stood next to the stout, red-faced, piggy-eyed man that was Constable Larch. They fumbled with the ebony sticks at their belt. The sticks had gold lettering that said "WP" and a coat of arms with a blue shield held up by two ducks and topped by a goat rearing up. (The coat of arms of the Twistle family, of course.)

You can still see one of these truncheons in Wildpool Museum today. It is inside a locked glass case. Not only does the case keep the dust off it but it also stops school children taking hold of it and using it to play rounders. The trouble is there is a human skull in the next case that would make a perfect ball. Museums would be much more fun if they allowed truncheon-and-skull rounder games, wouldn't they?

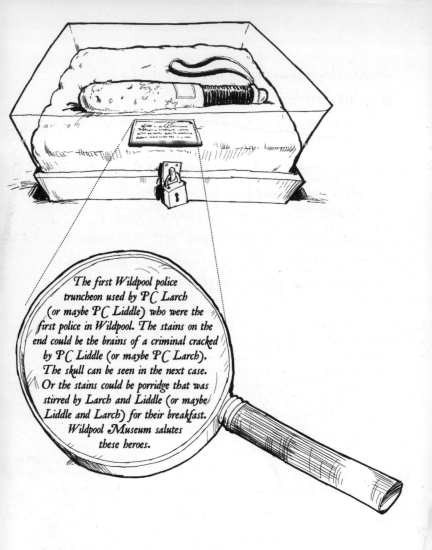

The first Wildpool police truncheon used by PC Larch (or maybe PC Liddle) who were the first police in Wildpool. The stains on the end could be the brains of a criminal cracked by PC Liddle (or maybe PC Larch). The skull can be seen in the next case. Or the stains could be porridge that was stirred by Larch and Liddle (or maybe Liddle and Larch) for their breakfast. Wildpool Museum salutes these heroes.

They wore matching uniforms of navy blue with silver buttons. Of course the police in the capital had

worn uniforms like this for five years but Lady Twistle drew her own design for the boys in blue of Wildpool.

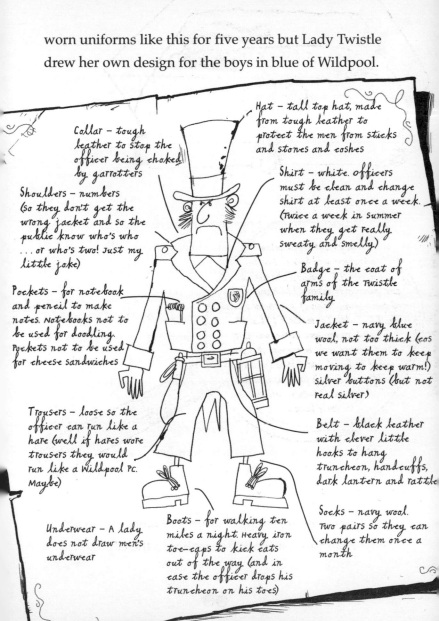

Collar – tough leather to stop the officer being choked by garrotters

Hat – tall top hat, made from tough leather to protect the men from sticks and stones and coshes

Shirt – white. Officers must be clean and change shirt at least once a week. (Twice a week in summer when they get really sweaty and smelly)

Shoulders – numbers (so they don't get the wrong jacket and so the public know who's who ... or who's two! Just my little joke)

Badge – the coat of arms of the Twistle family

Pockets – for notebook and pencil to make notes. Notebooks not to be used for doodling. Pockets not to be used for cheese sandwiches

Jacket – navy blue wool, not too thick (cos we want them to keep moving to keep warm!) silver buttons (but not real silver)

Trousers – loose so the officer can run like a hare (well if hares wore trousers they would run like a Wildpool PC. Maybe)

Belt – black leather with clever little hooks to hang truncheon, handcuffs, dark lantern and rattle

Underwear – A lady does not draw men's underwear

Boots – for walking ten miles a night. Heavy iron toe-caps to kick cats out of the way (and in case the officer drops his truncheon on his toes)

Socks – navy wool. Two pairs so they can change them once a month

Of course in the twentieth century you expect to hear a policeman blowing his whistle to call for help and tell the world there is a peace-breaker on the prowl. But those old policemen used wooden rattles to clatter out their warnings. If they lost their truncheons they could give the criminal a battle with the rattle! You can't do that with a whistle, can you? Rattles are a sad loss if you ask me.

Wildpool's new boys in blue were ready to rattle and roll down the steep streets and awful alleys, catching criminals and righting wrongs, beating beggars and locking up law-breakers.

If PCs Liddle and Larch looked scared stiff it was only because they didn't like standing on the stage being stared at by huge crowds (of ten or more). Once they were rambling down the roads they'd be fine.

Probably.

The constables had stepped out of a small room leading off from the council chamber. If we could look through the old oak door we would see a man in there. A large man. A very l-a-r-g-e man, not much wider than the door or heavier than a carthorse. He called himself Police Inspector Beadle.

Police Inspector Beadle did not wear a uniform. Police Inspector Beadle's fat face was not a face the people of Wildpool would see on the streets. That was the job of Larch and Liddle.

Police Inspector Beadle wore a plain suit of dark grey, a white shirt with a starched collar that was almost lost in the rolls of fat around his neck.

He tapped the pages of the report in front of him.

WILDPOOL POLICE FORCE

REPORT

Date: *3 January 1837*

PC Septimus Liddle (PC 01) and PC Archibald Larch PC 02) signed on today.

Liddle is thin, ancient and not very bright.

Larch is heavy, slow and as bright as a dark lantern.

They will do the job we need.

Police Inspector Beadle

Police Inspector Beadle smiled softly, folded the report and slipped it inside his jacket.

In the council chamber the mayor, who was only just taller than a gnome, stretched out an arm and pointed to the door. "What are you waiting for? Get out there and fight crime!"

Lady Twistle tugged angrily at his coat tails and rustled a piece of paper under his nose. "Read this, Ossie, the way I told you."

"Sorry, dear." Sir Oswald Twistle cleared his throat and squeaked the words. "Go forth into the jaws of terror, my brave lads!" Then he read the epic poem his wife had written for this great day.

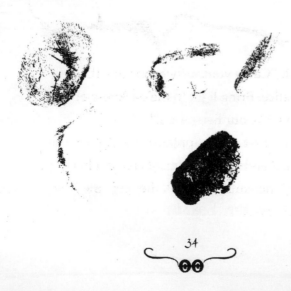

Fight for the right
By day and by night.
Go forth, and we bless you,
Though criminals test you.
Though they chase you with guns,
We know you won't run.
Though they chase you with knives,
We know you won't hide.
Go forth the world wide
We are there by your side...
...so to speak.

MONEY TALKS
Gold talks loudest!

He added, "Carry your truncheons like flaming torches of justice. Bring light to the darkness of our savage streets. Go, our heroes, go!"

The crowd burst out in applause. Mayor Twistle looked pleased and his wife almost cracked her make-up with her smile. "I think they like me," he whispered.

"I think they liked my speech," she huffed.

"Oh, yes dear. Sigh. Of course, dear. But one day they may like me. One day."

Constable Liddle turned his head stiffly in the hard leather collar and muttered under his moustache. "Chase us with guns? Police Inspector Beadle never said nothing about guns!"

Larch spoke out of the side of his fat mouth. "Police Inspector Beadle caught us stealing pennies from the little match-seller's tray. He said we'd go to prison if we didn't sign up for the police."

"Suppose so," sighed Liddle. "So let's get out there and catch some criminals."

"It's cold out there," Larch moaned.

"It's colder in Darlham Gaol cells."

"You're right. Let's get out there."

Shoulder-to-shoulder the two constables faced the crowd. They bent their knees and spoke with one voice, as Inspector Beadle had taught them. "Evening all!" Then they stepped from the stage and marched through the crowd who parted to form a sort of guard of honour. Someone opened the door and an icy blast of air struck their faces. The two men were almost in

step as they marched down the High Street.

"So let me get this right," Liddle said slowly. "The mayor wants us to set fire to our truncheons and use them as flaming torches?"

"No, Liddle. I don't think he meant us to do it really."

"That's good. That's really good."

"Why?"

"Cos I haven't any matches."

"Ah."

The green gas lamps glowed and lit the streets below them like a necklace of diamonds. Yellow light flared in the shipyards by the river. Hammers clanked on the new, steel steamship that would be one of the first in the world. It was called "The Pride of Wildpool".

I won't tell you how it got that name.

In the distance, across the river to the north, the fairground by the seashore lay dark and empty. On the higher ground to the south the mansions of the rich folk glittered smug and snug.

The railway trucks clattered and clanked while Locomotive No. 2 sparked and steamed. Coal trucks rattled down to the piers and tipped their black load into the waiting collier ships.

The piers were called 'drops' – if they had loaded lemons instead of coal I suppose they'd be lemon drops.

It was never quiet in Wildpool.

The constables looked around. "So? Where do we start?"

"We could walk down Low Street to the river?" Larch said.

Liddle gasped. "You're joking! That place is full of criminals! You won't catch me going down there at night!"

"Ah."

And so on that historic night the new Wildpool Police Force set out to fight for the right by day and by night.

But very carefully, of course.

Chapter 3

SACKS OF SWAG

Snow was falling as Smiff stepped out of his house the next morning.

Well, you didn't think the snow would be rising, did you?

His mother had done as Samuel Dreep asked and bought Smiff a new pair of boots. He even wore a pair of warm woollen socks.

Smiff marched up the steep hill, past the terrace of pitifully poor houses that made up Low Street. Many had boards across the windows to keep out

the draughts. Glass cost too much for the poor of Wildpool, even though there was a glass factory just at the first bend of the Wildpool river.

Samuel Dreep waited for Smiff at the top of the hill, and was wrapped in a fine scarf of red and white stripes. He wore black leather gloves and that shabby top hat as tall as a stove pipe. His boots were of the finest leather. Almost a gentleman, in fact.

"Good morning, Smiff," he said with a smile. "I hope you slept well?"

"A bit cold," Smiff shuddered.

"Soon you and your mother will be able to afford some good blankets to get her through to spring," Dreep promised, then spread his thin fingers wide. "If you do well at school, of course. But you will eat and sleep at the school."

Dreep turned and led the way through the snow-blown streets. Men and women hurried to work, heads down and collars turned up. The snow was white, the soot-stained walls of the houses, factories and shops were black, the faces of the people were grey. It looked like one of those moving pictures you see at the cinema these days ... though cameras had not been invented back in 1837, as you know.

Dogs jogged in search of rats to eat, but the rats were hiding warm in their holes too deep for dogs to dig them out.

"Good morning officers!" Dreep called across the mud-slushed, horse-clopped, cartwheel-slopped cobbles

Smiff looked up sharply. Two men in navy uniforms with high hats shivered in the shelter of the soap-factory wall. "Mornin' all!" they said with a stiff-jointed bend of the knees.

"May I take this chance to wish you the very best of luck with your new jobs, Constables."

Liddle and Larch gave frozen-lipped smiles. "Thank you sir."

"Who are they?" Smiff hissed.

"The enemy," Dreep said softly.

Dreep and Smiff soon arrived at a rambling and shambling house. It had once been a fine town house of a ship owner. But Wildpool grew. The huddle of houses on the riverside spread up the hill and streets like Low Street were thrown up.

When I say "thrown up" I don't mean vomited. They were thrown together in a hurry and were slums as soon as they were finished. They were slimy and smelly. So maybe I do mean like vomit.

Soon the ship owner could see shoddy slums at the corner of his road. He could smell the corpse-scented homes. He moved out to the hill beyond the south edge of the town. The part where all his rich friends lived.

His old house had been saved from the hammers of the wreckers. Now, a sign hung on the green gates.

MASTER CROOK'S
CRIME ACADEMY
Tuition for the children of the poor to help them stay out of prison.

And that was true, in a way! Master Crook would teach them so well they would never be caught – they would stay out of prison. (Darlham Gaol was a hateful place ten miles to the south. You wouldn't want to spend time in there.)

Behind the green academy gate was a small garden with a winter-withered tree and a tall, black-brick house with a newly painted door – a red door that matched Dreep's scarf.

Dreep took out a key and unlocked the door. "We usually keep the door locked . . . there are a lot of thieves about," he said, looking hard at Smiff.

"Very funny, I think not," Smiff said.

They stepped into a hall with a floor that shone with polish and stamped the light snow off their boots on to a mat.

The house had been a school for just one day but already it smelled like a school.

You may be unlucky enough to go to school. In that case you will know the smell I mean. All schools smell like a mix of wooden desks, teachers' mouldering breath and chalk dust – always chalk dust. Even after the last child has escaped from the last school they will still smell the same.

The doors were painted cream and the walls were painted a muddy shade of yellow. A new noticeboard had been nailed to the wall. It only had one notice on it.

MASTER CROOK'S CRIME ACADEMY

SCHOOL RULES

Pupils must ...

1 Run in ye corridors at all times
2 Be late for ye lessons
3 Disobey ye teachers
4 Write on ye school walls
5 Shout ye out aloud
6 Cheat in ye tests
7 Eat in ye class
8 Pick ye nose and eat ye it
9 Damage ye books or carve ye names on ye desks.

BUT:

10 Pupils must **NOT** pick on other pupils. No matter how weedy and worthless a classmate looks they all have a place at Master Crook's. Be warned. Bully not or ye shall be bullied.

"Huh!" Smiff sniffed. "Master Crook likes to say 'ye'."

"Yes, ye does," Dreep agreed.

Smiff stepped into a large room with a fine, high ceiling. Plaster angels with plaster horns to their lips looked down. A small coal fire burned in an iron fireplace and warmed the room. The windows looked out across the river to the north side of the town and the snow-capped hills.

There were five desks in the room and they faced a blackboard. But there was just one pupil sitting there. A girl as thin as Smiff but with curly fair hair and blue eyes like a doll. But she was dressed like Smiff – trousers and shirt, waistcoat and jacket, all a grim grey colour. She glared at Smiff (grimly).

"Meet Alice White," Dreep said. "Your first partner in crime."

"Pleased to meet—" Smiff began.

Alice cut in, "He doesn't look much of a criminal to me. I've seen deadlier dog droppings than him."

"Thank you, Alice, but Smiff is a skilled young thief," Dreep began to explain.

"Hah! Who says? You says?" the girl snorted. "So if he is so-o skilled, what's he doing here, eh? If he is so-o-o-o skilled he has nothing to learn. He's wasting his so-o-o-o-o skilled time, isn't he?"

Dreep pulled off his gloves and red scarf and laid them on a table at the front. "He just thinks too small," he explained. "We want to help him – and you – rob

the rich to feed the poor."

"Or rob the rich and get hanged for it . . . if skinny Smiff is as useless as he looks," the girl said and gave a sudden, savage, small-toothed smile.

"Alice. . ." Dreep said quietly. "You are not much of a big-time criminal yourself, are you?"

"No, well, yes, well, I made a living—"

Dreep cut in and said, "Alice was trying the Lucifer Dodge, weren't you?"

"Huh! So what? So what?"

"What's that?" Smiff asked.

The tall teacher stroked his fine moustache and explained. "A child takes a tray full of matches to sell on the street. As a rich gent walks past she spills them as if he's knocked them out of her hand. She scrabbles on the ground to pick them up and howls her little heart out. If the gent doesn't give her money then other people passing by may cough up a coin or two."

"So she gets paid for matches without selling them?" Smiff said.

"That's right. In fact she sells them over and over again. She gets her little friends to gather up the matches and try it again . . . and again."

"I make shillings a day," she argued.

"And we will teach you to make sovereigns a day," Dreep promised.

Alice opened her mouth to argue but Dreep went on, "Now meet your first teacher," he said and walked to a door that seemed to lead into the next room.

"Master Crook?" Smiff gasped.

"Ha! No, Master Crook is too busy finding new teachers and new pupils, making plans and setting up dodges. No, we have been very lucky. We have found one of the best burglars in the whole country." Dreep threw the door open and cried, like a showman in a circus ring. "Step forward, Bert!"

A round man rolled into the room. A man older than Smiff's mother with a face full of stubble . . . not at all like Smiff's mother. He had a white jersey with black stripes around it.

Or it could have been a black jersey with white stripes around it. In the tricky world of crime it could have been white with black OR black with white. That sort of thing is SURE to confuse the police. Remember this when you next plan to burgle a bungalow or filch from a flat.

He wore a black mask over his eyes but with eyeholes cut out so he could see. He carried a sack with "Swag" written on it. He looked a bit like a burglar really.

"I'm a burglar," Bert said proudly.

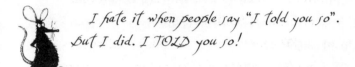

I hate it when people say "I told you so". But I did. I TOLD you so!

"I didn't think you were a jockey," Alice sneered. "Too fat by half."

"Potatoes," Bert sighed. "They was my downfall. I love potatoes. But they make you fat if you eat too many."

"Lor' you must eat a sack a day to get like that," the blonde girl giggled.

Dreep coughed gently. "Can we get on with the lesson, please, Alice?"

"S'pose so," she shrugged.

But once Bert the Burglar started talking Alice forgot her malice and listened like a cat at a mouse-hole.

Bert told them some of the rules that saw him safely through a life of crime and Alice licked her lips at the thought of how she could copy.

"But that was the old days," Bert said. "You have a new problem. We just had to dodge the old night-watch patrols. Watchmen was just ordinary family men taking turns at watching the streets. Easy to dodge them – or bribe them to set you free if you got caught. You have to deal with some new law officers." The burglar lowered his voice and it shook a little. "Police!"

"I've seen them!" Smiff cried.

"There you go! They have their eye on you even before you've started!" Bert moaned. "New laws need new tricks. Now, how are we going to deal with this force of highly trained, tough and ruthless men who can't be bribed?"

"Easy," Alice said. "There's only two of them. Send them off to some other part of town while you burgle a mile away."

Dreep patted his hands together. "Well done, Alice. I can see you are going to be a star pupil."

"I was going to say that," Smiff sniffed.

"Yeah, well you didn't, rat-face," Alice snapped. "I said it. I am going to be the brains in this team. You can carry the loot."

Smiff didn't have an answer to that so he gave it, ". . .!"

Bert the Burglar went on for an hour and gave them all his top tips. "Don't go in the front door, of course. You'll be seen in the light of the street. Slip round the back gate. Up the garden and in the back door."

"What if it's locked?" Smiff asked.

"I was going to say that," Alice objected.

"Yeah, well you didn't, cat-face," Smiff smirked.

"I will teach you how to open locks with a skeleton key," Bert promised. "And Master Crook has the most amazing plan. A scheme to tell you which houses will be empty."

"Great!" Smiff grinned.

"Of course you have to make sure. . ." Bert began. But Dreep heard the clock chime twelve and stopped him. Big mistake.

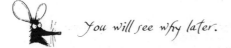 *You will see why later.*

"After lunch," Dreep said. He led the way to a large kitchen at the back of the school where hot soup was bubbling away on an open fire and a fresh white loaf of bread stood on the table.

Smiff had never seen so much food and he ate till

he was stuffed. "Pig," Alice muttered as she sipped at her soup like a lady.

After a pot of tea they went back to the classroom and spent an hour learning to pick locks. Then Bert went on to list some of the things they should be looking for.

MASTER CROOK'S CRIME ACADEMY
BURGLAR BERT'S TOP TIPS

Small and preshus is best - one jewel is wurf a fowzand copper pans . . . and it is a lot eezier to carry.

- **Metal** is for meltin - you cant sell gold cannlesticks but you can melt em down and sell the gold they is made of. Same with silver orneements.

- **Cutlery** is all right - nives, fawks and spoons sell well. But they rattle about when you carry them off. Carefull what you pinch.

- **China** is pretty uzeless - it chips and breaks and is hard to sell.

- **Cash** - well, coppers and sovrins are nice if you see some lying around.

Posh people use bank notes these days. But you cant spend em. No one would take a bank note off a poor person like you. Notes is trubble.

- **Clothes** – we all like a bit a silk or some nice sheets or blankerts. But they can be hard to hide. Have you seem them hoops those ladys have in their skirts?

- **Candels** – Wax candels, not the mutton fat ones that smell when they burn. Eezy to sell is candels. Stick em in.

- **Paintins** – hard to carry, imposserbull to sell cos they is ooneek. Try selling one and its a short cut to jail. Forget em – even the pretty puppy pitchers that you love.

* Last – don't get greadie. Fill up yer bag and leg it out as fast as yer can. Take it from one what nose.

"I hope you are a better burglar than you are a speller!" Alice jeered.

"Meaning. That's all that matters," Bert argued. "You get my meaning, don't yer? So button your cheeky little lip and take a telling."

Alice pouted. She pushed out her bottom lip – but

she didn't have a button to button it with. In fact she didn't have a button-hole in the other lip either. So she pouted instead.

Now it's all very well being cheeky to your teacher. Teachers can take it. That is what they get paid to do. The problem is you may upset your teacher a bit.

An upset teacher is a bad teacher.

And Burglar Bert was a bad teacher that afternoon. He taught the two students almost everything he knew . . . but not quite everything. He forgot something. The thing he was going to tell them when the lunch break clock had chimed.

If Alice hadn't been cheeky about his spelling he may have remembered. But she was, and he didn't.

That's why Alice and Smiff make a terrible mistake. A mistake that might cost them their short little lives.

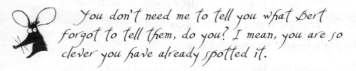

You don't need me to tell you what Bert forgot to tell them, do you? I mean, you are so clever you have already spotted it.

But Smiff didn't see the flaw in the plan. Even smart little, curly-haired, blue-eyed, big-brained Alice didn't spot it.

Oh dear. Oh dear, oh dear, oh dear!

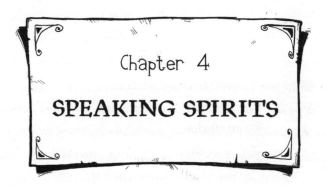

Chapter 4

SPEAKING SPIRITS

The two new students at Master Crook's Crime Academy went back to the school kitchen. They shared a pot of tea and scones.

"Is this real butter?" Smiff gasped.

"Yes, and real plum jam," Alice added, spreading the sticky purple mess thickly over her scone.

"What's jam?" the boy asked.

"Mmf-mmf nn Mmmmf!" Alice answered with a mouth full of scone.

As you know this means "Try it and see".
Please don't speak with your mouth full like this

charmless child just did. You could spit crumbs all over your feet. Passing pigeons could then swoop down and attack those crumbs, pecking your feet till you bled to death. Remember: speaking with your mouth full kills.

Smiff tried it and drooled at the sweetness. "Ooooh! That's nice!" he said. He'd never tasted jam before, not even when his father was at home and bringing in money. Dripping fat – the grease off mutton chops – was the richest thing Smiff ever got to spread on his bread.

Samuel Dreep nodded as he stood by the fire, polishing his hat. "That's the sort of food you can have in your house if you work hard. Tender beef, pork pies, fruit jellies and sugared candies. Work hard and you'll be fat as a cat in a mouse-filled house."

"When do we start?" Smiff asked.

"As soon as you've finished tea," Dreep said and his green eyes glowed in the amber light of the fire. "Today is the first day of the rest of your life," he said.

"And the last day if we get caught," Smiff sniffed. "So where do we start?"

"In the Apollo music hall," the man told him.

APOLLO MUSIC HALL, WILDPOOL

SOLE LESSEE MR FARLAND PROUDLY PRESENTS

A GRAND VOCAL INSTRUMENTAL THESPIAN AND TERPSICHOREAN FESTIVAL

WEDNESDAY 4TH. JANUARY 1837 AT 8:00 P.M.

FOR THIS NIGHT ONLY MR EDWARD EDWARDS
HAS KINDLY AGREED TO RECITE
"IF MOTHER COULD SEE ME NOW"

THE HIGHLAND DANCERS
Will dance to the pipes of Mackay Mackee

MISS NELLIE SHERRIE
Sentimental vocalist, ballads and opera to bring tears to your eyes

SCREAMING EXTRAVAGANZA DE RAY, MUNSTER AND ECCLES
With their amazing talking elephant

MADAME BOER'S PERFORMING DOGS AND MONKEYS

JOVIAL JOE JONES
With completely new comic songs including
"La-di-da, He's the pet of all the ladies"

THE WILDPOOL PANTOMIME PLAYERS
Will perform Little Jack and the big beanstalk with amazing giant

AND TONIGHT'S GUEST STAR
THE SPIRIT MASTER WILL ENTER YOUR MIND AND
READ YOUR SECRET THOUGHTS. ASTOUNDING!

Admission: Boxes 1 shilling; Balcony 9 pence; Stalls 6 pence; Back seats 4 pence
Entertainment will start at 8:00p.m. doors will open half an hour earlier
No dogs, no drinking your own drink, no spitting and ladies are not allowed
to smoke. Food and drink are served at the intervals, before and after the show

"How does this help us to burgle a house?" Smiff asked.

"You'll see," Dreep said. "There is one act there who will help. We will go along and see him after we have made our first call. A call on our friends, the police!"

Alice had swallowed her second scone and washed it down with steaming tea. She almost choked on it now. "Police? Aren't they the new law in town?"

"They are, Alice. Two finer men you couldn't wish to see . . . in a zoo. Smiff and I met them this morning." He looked up at the clock on the kitchen wall. "Six o'clock? They will be in the new police station now, writing up their reports of last night's duty. They won't set out to patrol the town till after eight tonight."

"You mean we have to do our burglary and be back here before eight?"

"No. We can't do that because the rich folk won't leave their houses till almost eight," Dreep explained.

"So . . . if we can't burgle before eight and we can't burgle after eight then when do we get to do the job?"

"After eight."

"But the new police blokes will be out. They could catch us with bags full of stolen swag."

"But you have already thought of that, remember?" Dreep asked. "Send them off to some other part of town while you burgle a mile away, you said."

"So I did," Alice nodded. "Cracking idea, though I say it myself."

"You will go to the police station and you will tell them about the burglary that will take place tonight."

"We don't know where that will be yet, do we?"

"We know it will be somewhere on the South Hill side of town."

"So we send them anywhere but there?"

"It's what the gentlemen who go shooting call a 'decoy'. You will tell them there is to be a burglary far away from the place we plan to burgle. They will go to watch the decoy place. We will know they are safely out of the way."

Alice nodded. Then she frowned. "Why can't Smiff do it?"

Dreep nodded. "You, Alice, are a good little actress. You put on a wonderful act when you pretended to spill your matches in the street. And, of course, the

59

police constables saw Smiff with me this morning. They are not the brightest buttons in the boot box but they may just remember him. You will wear a cap – pretend to be a boy. Then, if things do go wrong. . ."

"Wrong?"

"They won't – but if they do we just stick you in a dress and the boy who gave them the decoy dummy has vanished!"

"All right," Alice agreed. "What do I do?"

And Samuel Dreep told her.

Half an hour later she walked into the building next door.

"Evenin' all!" Liddle and Larch said, looking over the counter at the soot-stained face of a "boy" in a flat cap.

"Evenin' all," Alice said. "Can I speak to the officer in charge, please?"

Liddle pulled himself up to his full but skinny height. "That would be Inspector Beadle . . . but he never sees anyone. Maybe Constable Larch and me can be of assistance?"

Alice sucked air sharply between her teeth. "Ooooh! I don't know! I have information so-o

60

important, so-o-o-o secret I could be chopped into a thousand tiny pieces for telling you. We are dealing with very dangerous criminals here!"

"Ah," Liddle nodded. "In that case Constable Larch will deal with it. He's not afraid of dangerous criminals, are you Larch?"

"Yes."

Alice shook her head, "Well . . . dangerous for children."

"Children?"

"About my age."

"Oh!" Liddle laughed. "We aren't afraid of kids. What are they up to? Throwing stones at the railway engine? Pinching socks off washing lines?" he chuckled.

"Or worse!" Larch laughed. "Knocking on doors and running away!" The two men roared with laughter.

Foolish men. They don't know what you and I know. If a kid nicks your pocket watch then the watch stays as nicked as if my granny had taken it. In fact there were so many thieving kids around in the 1870s they invented schools to get

*them off the streets! Never scoff at a thieving
child or you'll lose your watch... if you don't
watch it. Master Crook knew that.*

"Burglary," Alice said.

The men stopped laughing.

"Oh, that is serious!" Larch agreed.

"They could hang for it," Liddle nodded. "At
the very least they could be sent off to Australia for
fourteen years."

"At the very least. Cruel place, Australia. It's on the
other side of the world where people walk upside down."

"The blood would rush to your head!" Liddle cried.
"Terrible. You'd be better off getting hanged in the
comfort of your own town."

"Not that being hanged is what you'd call
comforta—"

"STOP!" Alice screamed. "Stop!"

The two men looked at her as if they had forgotten
she was there. "Evenin' all?" they said.

"At nine o'clock tonight two burglars will break
into the Wildpool hospital."

"Why? Are they sick?" Liddle asked.

"They wish to steal bottles of laudanum," Alice said quietly. "Posh people have nannies to bring up their children," she went on.

"I was brought up by a billy goat cos my parents couldn't afford a nanny!" Larch laughed. Alice glared. Larch said, "Sorry. Laudanum."

"Nannies give laudanum to babies to send them to sleep and shut them up so they can have a quiet life," she said.

"Or gin! That's good for babies," Larch said.

If you have a squalling baby brother or sister in your house please do NOT give it a spoonful of gin. The kindest way to deal with squalling babies is to take a large roll of cotton wool. Stick it in your ears. Problem solved. Don't thank me. It's all part of Mr X's service.

Alice said, "Nannies pay a sovereign for a bottle of laudanum. Catch the burglars at the hospital and make Inspector Beadle proud of you."

"And Mayor Twistle!" Larch said. "We could even get a medal. We'll be there. Outside the hospital. . ."

"Hiding in the bushes," Alice said. "Between eight

o'clock and ten o'clock."

"Eight and ten. We'll be there," Larch promised.

"Good," Alice said with a rare smile.

"Now, young man, there could be a reward if this leads to an arrest. Give us your name and address," Liddle said and picked up a pencil.

"No reward," Alice said in the voice of an angel. "I am proud just to serve my town and do my duty to Mayor Twistle."

The girl turned on her heel and ran from the station. Two constables looked after her. "What a noble young man," Liddle sighed. "Noblest of the noble. It gives us hope for the future of our world. If only all young people were as . . . as. . ."

"Noble?"

"Noble."

"Reminded me of someone," Liddle said, sucking on the end of his drooping white moustache.

"Reminded ME of the little match girl we nicked pennies from," Larch muttered. "But he couldn't be."

"Impossible," Liddle agreed.

"Anyway, the lad's information means we'll have two arrests tonight. Inspector Beadle will be pleased!"

Larch chortled.

"Who's the other one?" Liddle asked.

Larch pulled out the piece of paper from the back of the report book. "Orders from Inspector Beadle."

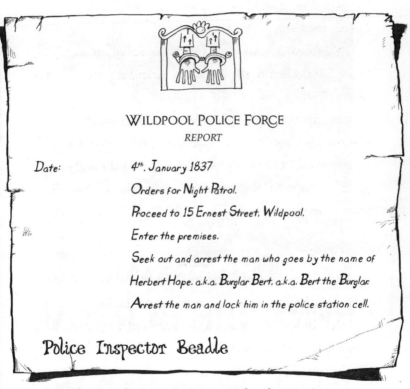

WILDPOOL POLICE FORCE
REPORT

Date:

4ᵗʰ. January 1837

Orders for Night Patrol.

Proceed to 15 Ernest Street, Wildpool.

Enter the premises.

Seek out and arrest the man who goes by the name of

Herbert Hope. a.k.a. Burglar Bert. a.k.a. Bert the Burglar.

Arrest the man and lock him in the police station cell.

Police Inspector Beadle

"Right, Larch, we've a busy night ahead of us. Better be off!"

WANTED

BERT THE BURGLAR
HAVE YOU SEEN THIS MAN?
10 GUINEAS REWARD
FOR ANY INFORMATION

Smiff Smith also had a busy night ahead of him. The snow was still more like frozen rain than the big fluffy flakes you see on Christmas cards. It blew across the cobbles and rattled against the ice puddles.

Smiff was happy in his new boots. Samuel Dreep led the way to the Apollo music hall, turned into a back lane from the side and went in through the stage door.

The doorkeeper looked up from his desk. "Can I help?" he asked and stroked his thick sideburns as if he were important.

"We have come to see your star. The Spirit Master," Dreep said as he brushed snow off his shoulders on to the doorkeeper's well-swept floor.

The man scowled but said, "Down the corridor. Third door on the right. The door with the star on it."

Dreep swept his hat off and gave a bow. Snow from the hat scattered on the floor. He marched along the corridor. Smiff's nose picked up a rich mix of smells – sweet perfume from the dancing girls, greasepaint and powder from the actors and ale and cigar smoke from where the audience would be sitting.

"Where's the elephant?" he asked. "I can't smell elephant?"

"It's a trick. It's a girl in an elephant's costume," Dreep explained then knocked on the door with a silver star on it.

"Come!" came a booming voice from inside.

The visitors stepped inside. The Spirit Master stood there. A handsome man with blazing brown eyes and long dark hair swept back from his forehead. "Good evening. . ." Dreep began.

The Spirit master raised a hand. Dreep fell silent. The showman looked at Smiff. "Careful, boy, I can read your mind!"

"I hope not!" Smiff squawked.

"You have a curious name . . . I see a name beginning with 'S' . . . stiff . . . skiff . . . Smiff!"

"Amazing!" Smiff gasped.

"I see a steep row of houses . . . poor houses. And a woman . . . a woman with a cupboard full of mop buckets . . . this woman . . . is your mother. . ."

"Yes, my mother IS a woman!" the boy cried in wonder.

"And you have just changed jobs . . . you were a shop-thief but now you are going for greater things . . . burgling fine houses, I think."

"That is incredible!" Smiff choked. "If you can read everyone's mind like that . . . why . . . there would be no crime! You'd just tell the police what all the villains are thinking. We're done for, Mr Dreep! Done for!"

Dreep threw back his head and laughed. He looked at the Spirit Master and said, "Knock it off, George. Save the mind-reading for the audience."

"But Mr Dreep . . . he CAN read minds. He knows all about me!" Smiff insisted.

Dreep shook his head. "He can not read minds. He knows all about you because I told him all about you last night after I met you. It's all a trick."

"It fooled me," Smiff said angrily.

Well, you can't blame Smiff. You would be angry if someone made you look stupid. Or you might be angry. I mean some people look stupid from the day they are born! Look in a mirror and you might spot one of those people! Hah! Only joking.

George, the Spirit Master, didn't look too happy either. "Oh, Samuel, you have to spoil things, don't you?"

"Sorry, George." He turned to the boy. "The truth is George does have a wonderful act. He guesses things about people and amazes them. He also has the most wonderful memory. He sees someone once and he remembers everything about them. He can answer every question that the audience call out to him. And that's how he can help us!"

Smiff was interested now. "How can he help us?"

Dreep explained. "Many of the rich folk of Wildpool will come along to see the show. George will look out into the audience and he will recognize a lot of the faces. If those people are here tonight then they are not at home!"

"Those are the homes we can burgle! I get it!" Smiff cried. "Oh, but how does Spirit Master tell us? I mean he can't say . . . 'I see we have Mr and Mrs Jones here tonight from 71 Frith Road. Pop off and burgle their house, Smiff.' I mean he can't!"

"No," Dreep agreed. "He will use a secret code. Tell us, George."

And George the Spirit Master told the boy exactly how the code would work.

Chapter 5

LIGHT OF LIME

Liddle and Larch stepped into the cold street. They clattered along with truncheons and handcuffs, lanterns and rattles all swinging from their belts. A deaf thief would hear them coming two miles away.

They marched, in step, past the darkened house next to the police station . . . a house with a red door and a sign that read, "Master Crook's Crime Academy".

"Did you lock the door behind us?" Larch asked.

"Nah! I think Inspector Beadle is still in the building."

Larch nodded. "We don't see much of him, do we?

Since he gave us the jobs, I mean."

"He spends a lot of time in his office. He is plotting to overthrow the criminal musty minds of Wildpool."

"I think you will find that is 'master' minds," Larch said. "Anyway he was in there when we went home to bed this morning."

"Was he?"

"I could hear his clock ticking in the office."

"Ah!"

"And he was there when we signed on duty tonight!" Larch said.

"Clock ticking again?"

"That's right." Larch stopped and shook snow off his boots. "Here! Maybe he never went home. Maybe he sleeps in the station."

"Caw!" Liddle cawed. "What a man."

"No! No! No-o!" Larch said. "Remember who it is who goes out into the night, arrests burglars, hides in bushes, nabs thieves. Who's that?"

"Dunno."

"You and me, Liddle. You and ME!"

"True. But we haven't arrested anybody. Not yet."

"Aha! But we are just about to," Larch told him.

"Ah," Liddle nodded. His cheeks were being whipped by his wispy white moustache waving in the wind. He stepped on the legs of a blind beggar who lay in the shelter of a shop doorway.

"Here!" the beggar called. "Watch where you're walking!"

"Watch where you're lying!" Liddle shouted back.

"How can I watch anything when I'm blind?"

"Suppose you have a point," Liddle nodded. "Sorry. Evenin' all."

"Good evening Constable," the beggar said with a sad smile.

The constables reached the end of Ernest Street. Just like Low Street, a few roads along, it sloped down steeply to the river. Women in shawls and wooden clogs slithered up to the shops at the top. Larch and Liddle's big boots, with steel studs, skidded and sparked as they stepped carefully down. Liddle counted, "One . . . two . . ." until he reached ". . . fifteen. Here we are, Larch. The house of Bert the Burglar."

"Are you sure?" Larch asked.

"There's no number on the door," Liddle said.

73

"Ooooh! We don't want to go barging in, hitting people with our truncheons, handcuffing them up and dragging them back to the station if they're the wrong people, do we?"

"I see the problem," Liddle said. "Tell you what . . . if there is a bloke inside we'll come right out and ask him. 'Are you Bert the Burglar?' we'll ask him."

"Clever, Liddle. Very clever. I can see why you got the job," Larch chuckled.

"Let's hope this is the right number," Liddle muttered. "We haven't got all night to search all the houses. We have to get across the river to the hospital," Liddle said. "I mean I THINK I counted right.

The truth is he had run out of fingers to count on when he reached ten. I would be the same, I don't know about you. Anyway, he tried to use his toes but they were froze together. If you have two toes froze together, do they count as one? I don't knows.

People should get numbers put on their doors, you know. Instead of these stupid little signs."

"Sign?" Larch asked. "What sign? What does it say?"

Liddle's dark lantern had a narrow slot in the front to let out the light but keep out the wind. He shone it on the sign.

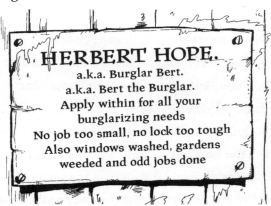

HERBERT HOPE.
a.k.a. Burglar Bert.
a.k.a. Bert the Burglar.
Apply within for all your
burglarizing needs
No job too small, no lock too tough
Also windows washed, gardens
weeded and odd jobs done

"What's 'a.k.a.'?" he asked.

"Also known as," Larch explained.

"Nah! That would be 'a.n.a.'," Liddle argued. "Still this looks like the place."

"I wouldn't trust that sign," Larch scoffed. "If he's a burglar he could be lying! He might really live next door! That's what I would do if I were a burglar."

"Let's give it a shot," Liddle said and rapped on the door with his truncheon.

"What did you do that for?" Larch asked.

"I didn't want to hurt me knuckles," Liddle told him.

"No! I mean why are we knocking? We're the police on the trail of a criminal. We should just march in. Catch him by surprise."

"Right then," Liddle said.

"Oh, it's too late NOW," Larch groaned.

"Who's there?" a voice asked from behind the door.

"Police. Open in the name of the law!" Larch roared.

The door opened. "Evening!" Bert said brightly.

"Bert the Burglar?"

"That's me."

"We arrest you in the name of the law," Larch said. He turned to Liddle. "Get out your notebook. . . Now Burglar Bert, a.k.a. Bert the Burglar, anything you say may be written down and used in court."

"Knickers!" Bert said.

"Pardon?"

"Knickers. Go on – take it down. I don't care," the old thief said happily.

"But we are going to lock you up for the night. You will appear in court in the morning."

Bert grinned, "Hang on while I get me coat. Looks chilly out there." He put on a heavy brown coat and

pulled on a large cap. "Right, lads. Off we go!"

He stepped on to Ernest Street, closed the door behind him and said, "Right, lads. Let's be off!"

The policemen struggled to keep up with the burglar as he walked up the street to the top and turned towards the police station. "You seem almost happy to be arrested," Larch panted.

"I don't mind, son," Bert shrugged. "I have never done a crime in Wildpool so you'll have to let me go . . . but while I am in your police cell I can't be out burgling places. If somewhere gets burgled tonight then you can't blame me. So, come on, let's get to that cell and I hope you have a nice coal fire on there and a cup of tea."

Larch jogged to keep up with Bert. "What burglary?" he asked. "You mean the hospital job?"

"Ah!" Bert cried happily. "You heard about that then? It's the talk of the town, isn't it? The sooner you lock me up the sooner you can get off to catch them in the act."

Bert began to whistle as he marched past Master Crook's Crime Academy and straight through the front door of the police station. He walked into the cell, slammed the door shut behind him then took out a

piece of wire. By the time Liddle and Larch had caught up, the old man had used the wire to make a skeleton key and lock the door. "It's all right, lads, I'll light the fire myself. I'll be snug and warm while you two go and freeze in the hospital hedge. Have a nice night!"

Liddle and Larch looked at one another. They were quite pleased to have made their first arrest. But there was something wrong about it. Something neither man could put his finger on.

"Do you think," Larch said, "we should tell Inspector Beadle we have a suspect in the cells?"

Liddle nodded. "Good idea. I mean . . . he'll be in charge of the building while we are out with our truncheons of crime, fighting fires."

"Truncheons of fire, fighting crime, you mean," Larch said.

They stood at the top of the stairs leading down to the basement. "His clock's ticking," Liddle said.

"You go down first," Larch said.

Liddle stuck out his chin and walked carefully down the wooden staircase. He tapped on the navy blue door at the bottom.

"Enter!" said the deep but soft voice.

The large shape of the inspector was planted on a chair. Wobbling bits of fatness seemed to spill over. The inspector's sharp eyes made the constables nervous. The clock tick sounded like a horse's hoof on an iron roof.

And the clock tock sounded just as loud. Of course you don't often hear horses' hooves on iron roofs – maybe you have NEVER heard them. In that case I will have to ask you to imagine it. For I have only heard it once. "Clip-clop, clip-clop, slip-drop, neigh-splatt." You do NOT want to know what happened.

Liddle spoke quickly. "We have arrested the suspect Burglar Bert a.k.a. Bert the Burglar and have locked him in the cells above, and all he'll say is 'knickers' and we are now on our way to the hospital to catch a burglar who is planning to steal bottles of laudanum that babies give to nannies so they can have a quiet life and we'll arrest them and bring them back and put them in the other cell."

Inspector Beadle nodded slowly, making his chins wobble. He pushed a piece of paper over the desk. "Here is a map of the hospital," he said softly. "You will need it. I have marked the laudanum store with an 'x'

and the hedge where you can hide with a 'p'," he said.

"A 'p'?"

"It's a privet hedge."

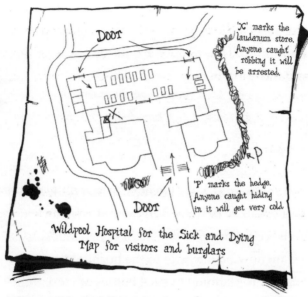

Constable Liddle picked up the map and slipped it inside his notebook. "Fear not, sir, we will arrest them with our flaming truncheons." He raised his truncheon high above his head.

"Good man," the inspector said softly. "I can see I was right to give you this job. Now go and do it."

Liddle gave a sharp salute and cried, "Yes, sir, ouch!"

He cried "ouch" because he had forgotten he was holding a truncheon in his saluting hand. Don't feel too sorry for him. His helmet saved him cracking his skull.

The officers rattled up the stairs and out into the night once more. They headed for the bridge over the river and the north bank.

Of course YOU know that the burglary will take place on the south side of the river. But you only know that because I told you. So don't be too pleased with your cleverness.

After all, you have not worked out how the Spirit Master will get the message to Alice and Smiff, have you? To find that out we need to return to the music hall. . .

The front doors were open now and people were starting to enter from the street. Alice had joined Smiff and they sat in the back row of the theatre seats with Samuel Dreep.

Gentlemen were taking their seats and lighting cigars. They carried glasses of ale from the theatre bar rooms at the back and chatted while they waited for the show to start.

Ladies in their best bonnets and warmest shawls

took their seats. They sipped at little glasses of sherry and gossiped behind the fans they carried.

As usual Alice found something to be angry about. "Four pence tickets at the back of the theatre. We will see nothing from here. What sort of seats do you call these, Mr Dreep? I can hardly even see the stage for the smoke. If I was the mayor I would ban smoking in places like this!"

Dreep spoke quietly. "Alice, you are not dressed as a rich young lady. You are dressed as an urchin boy. If you sat in the good seats at the front you would be in the middle of all the fine ladies in their ribbons and bows, satin gowns and lace bonnets. People would notice you. The best burglars are the ones who do not get themselves noticed."

Alice pouted. "Who says? You says?"

"And of course, once George, the Spirit Master, gives you the secret message you need to slip out of the theatre without being seen. If you are at the back you can do that easily."

Alice pouted some more. Smiff was too dazzled by the beauty of the theatre to notice his partner's mood. "How do they make that light?" he breathed. Brilliant

beams of blue and green swept across the stage as the stage managers practised.

"It's a new invention," Dreep said. "It's called lime-light. It's a gas light but not the same sort of gas they use in street lights. Wildpool is the first theatre in the country to have it outside the capital. It is so special they say the mayor himself will honour us with a visit this evening."

The theatre orchestra were starting to fill the "pit" in front of the stage and blow tunelessly into their instruments, or scrape at their violins to warm them up. Footlights at the front of the stage were lit and their red, yellow, green and blue shades threw a rainbow of light on to the dark stage curtains.

The chatter and laughter changed suddenly. It became an excited babble and the smoking men and gossiping women turned to look up to the rooms at the side that looked down on the stage and were very close to the stage. Little rooms called "boxes" that cost a whole shilling per seat to buy. Only the very rich went in there.

Alice, Smiff and Dreep followed the glances. They saw a large, white-faced, pink-cheeked, scarlet-lipped woman in a green gown like a ship's sail and a bonnet like a spread peacock's tail. She looked down on the

smoky masses below and raised a hand in a white silk glove. Just one wave. Then she sat down on her gold-framed seat with satin cushions.

Now the crowd could see the little man with the neat beard who had been standing behind her. He was in a fine black suit with a bow tie and white gloves too. He waved and waved and smiled at the people below.

"Mayor Twistle," Dreep explained. "Always likes to be seen out and about."

"Why?" Smiff asked.

"He wants the people of Wildpool to like him."

"And do they?"

Dreep snorted. "Twistle made his fortune from factories and lands. He used his money to buy the votes that made him mayor. But he will never, ever give money to the people who need it . . . the poor. In Twistle's world the poor would starve to death and leave the town for fine folk like him and his wife Arabella. No one likes Oswald Twistle."

"Except his wife," Smiff argued.

Dreep's great green eyes glittered in the limelight. "Especially not his wife!" he laughed. "In fact I would not be surprised if Master Crook didn't have a plan to

fix Sir Oswald."

"Fix? How?"

"I don't know. You never know with Master Crook."

Alice scowled, which made a change from the pout but not much of a change. "Will we get to meet this Master Crook?" she demanded. "I want to see him."

Dreep became serious. "You would NOT want to see him, Alice White. He is more terrible than the nastiest nightmare you have ever dreamed. But you WILL see him if you do something very wrong and upset him."

"You're scaring me," Smiff said.

"You don't scare ME!" Alice hissed. "In fact I don't even think Master Creepy Crook exists. I think YOU are Master Crook!" she went on.

Dreep turned his gooseberry eyes towards the stage where the orchestra had started playing a jolly tune. "Oh, is that what you think, Alice White?"

"Am I right?" she cried.

"Shush," said someone in front of her. "The show is about to start."

Alice shushed her mouth, but her mind was screaming with questions and anger.

Smiff sat next to her and felt the danger.

85

Chapter 6

MESSAGE OF MYSTERY

The orchestra played and the curtain rose. Limelight glittered on the bright faces of a group of singers who grinned at the audience as they sang from a sheet that was hung above the stage.

"It's so good to see you here,
We will bring you such good cheer;
We will bring you smiles and tears,
Tasty pies, refreshing beers!"

The audience sang along and laughed. Everyone was in a good mood and for a while even Alice forgot why they were really there. She sniffed away a tear when Mr Edward Edwards came on stage to sing, "If mother could see me now".

The truth is she wiped her nose on her sleeve. This is not a pleasant habit but if you can't afford a handkerchief what else can you do? Drip on to your lap? Snot a nice thought is it?

"What's wrong?" Smiff asked her.

"I've got a cold in my nose," she lied.

"The song upset you? If your mother could see you now she'd be proud of you," he said gently.

"Who says? You says? Yeah, well she's a bit too dead to see me, isn't she, dummy."

"Sorry."

"Forget it."

When the Highland dancers came on stage she did forget her misery as they whirled to the skirl of the bagpipes. A twirl of tartan to the stamping and clapping of the audience. They left the stage to roars and cheers.

Then the lights dimmed and the compere stood

in a small pool of limelight. "And now, ladies and gentlemen, the most awesome and amazing Apollo act you will ever see, even if you live to be two hundred years old!"

"Oooo!" the audience gasped.

"We proudly present a man with the power to step inside your mind, to read your every thought!"

"Oooo!"

The compere pointed suddenly at a lady in the third row. "So you'd better be careful what you think, young lady!"

"Ha! Ha! Ha!"

"Yes, this man speaks to the spirits of our dear dead friends."

"Oooo!"

"This is not some cheap stage magic trick . . . this is a mindboggling mystery of the universe, brought to you by the fabulously phenomenal, the terrifyingly talented, the confoundingly clever . . . Spirit Master!"

"Hooray!"

The curtains opened. Samuel Dreep's friend George stood in front of plain black painted boards. He wore pale make-up with heavy shadows around his eyes

and thin red lips. He said nothing for a few moments. The people in the audience all seemed to be holding their breath.

At last he spoke in a deep voice. "The spirits are with us tonight. There is someone in the audience . . . someone called Jenny!"

"That's me!" about ten women gasped.

"Your dead mother sends greetings across the universe. She is watching over you," the Spirit Master boomed.

"Ooooo!"

Smiff nodded. It was an easy trick . . . pick a common name and you could be sure half of the people with that name would have a dead parent.

But the next trick baffled Smiff. "I want three people to help me!" He pointed to the woman in the second row, "You, young lady?"

She giggled and nodded. He passed a piece of paper, an envelope and a pencil to her.

"Someone from the back, perhaps?"

Samuel Dreep stood up and called, "Me, Spirit Master!" He walked to the stage to collect the paper and pencil. Finally George turned his shadowy eyes

on the box by the stage. He handed a sheet to Lady Twistle. She smiled and took it. The Spirit Master said, "I want you to write down three words. Three words that mean something to you. Three words that I could not possibly guess. . ."

They each did as he told them, folded the papers and placed them in the envelopes. They handed them to him. The Spirit Master took an envelope. He held it to his forehead so it hid his eyes. The audience fell silent.

The Spirit Master spoke slowly. "These are the words of the young man from the back. . ."

The audience turned and looked at Dreep, then turned their eyes back to the stage. "The first word is . . . Crook . . . the second word is Academy . . . and the third word is . . . ah, this is so hard . . . I think you have spelled it wrong!"

The audience laughed.

"But the word seems to be S-m-i-f-f . . . Smiff?"

Dreep turned to the audience, "Amazing!"

George opened the envelope, took out the paper and said, "Crook, Academy and . . . Smiff!"

The audience cheered then fell silent again. "The

young lady's words are . . . Barney? A boyfriend perhaps?"

The audience laughed and the young lady blushed.

"The second word is . . . handbag? Maybe something you love more than Barney?"

Laughter.

"And the third word is something you love most of all . . . shoes! Am I right?" He opened the envelope and nodded as the girl cried, "I don't believe it!"

Finally he turned to the mayor's wife. "And you, my lady. . ." he pressed the envelope to his forehead and held it there longer than ever. "Ah! My lady, you are really testing me, aren't you? Trying to catch me out!"

Arabella Twistle raised her fan to hide her smirk. The Spirit Master's face twisted in pain as if he were trying to tear the words from the air. "The first word is . . . doodle . . . the second word is . . . humpty . . . and the third word is . . . is simply the letter X. Am I right?" He pulled the paper from the envelope and smiled as Lady Twistle gasped, "Amazing!"

George passed the papers to Dreep. "Can you check them? I haven't lied?"

"No . . . they are all correct . . . every word!" Dreep said, waving the papers excitedly at the audience.

They cheered as Dreep slipped the papers into his pocket and went back to his seat.

Dreep returned to his seat beside Smiff and Alice. "Can he really read minds?" Smiff asked quietly as George went on with the act.

Dreep explained, "No."

"So how does he do it?"

"He has a friend in the audience. The first words he gave out were mine."

"How did he know what you'd written?" Smiff hissed.

Alice answered. "They decided that before the show. Mr Dreep wrote what they agreed. Easy. Would only fool a dummy."

"But the girl? How did he know her words?"

Samuel Dreep shrugged. "He tore open the first envelope to read my words."

"Yes, I saw that."

"And THIS is what he read," Dreep said, passing the paper to Smiff. Smiff looked at the paper.

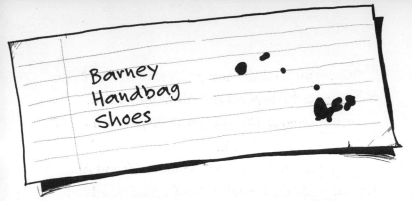

Barney
Handbag
Shoes

Smiff frowned. Dreep explained. "George really tore open the girl's envelope, read her words then pretended they were in my sealed envelope."

"I get it!" Smiff cried. "He gave the girl her words – said he was opening her envelope to check, but opened Lady Twistle's envelope and read it."

Doodle
Humpty
X

"Correct."

"He gave Lady Twistle the words then opened the last envelope, but that was really your envelope,"

Alice finished.

The boy looked at the third sheet.

Crime
Academy
Smiff

"He's a cheat and a crook," she said.

"Just like us," Smiff laughed.

And just like YOU. For, now you know how it
works you can try this trick yourself. If you are
really good then people will think you are in contact
with the afterlife. If you are really bad they will
probably throw rotten eggs and squidgy tomatoes at
you. But a life of tricks is a life of risks . . . as
Alice and Smiff were about to find out.

"Hush!" Dreep said. "This is the part of the show
where he gives us our message."

The Spirit Master was giving curious messages

to people in the audience. Messages from their dead friends and loved ones. Messages that were such a jumble the people had to make their own meanings.

"A graveyard cat is sobbing for its lost mistress, Juliet, and the toast on the table is burned."

"Yes!" a man cried. "I think that's my Uncle Will speaking to me!"

"Now!" the Spirit Master boomed. "I have a message for . . . Alice. A message from a long-lost friend."

"That's us," Samuel Dreep said softly. "Write down exactly what he says."

"Here is the message, Alice!" the man on stage cried and stared up into the lights as if a spirit was speaking to him from there. "The wind is slight tonight little Ellen . . . unlucky for some – so on until time halts. . . Dream richly, I value everything!"

George gave a nod to show he was finished. Dreep slipped from his seat and Smiff and Alice followed him out of the theatre. Smiff wanted to see the rest of the show. It was a world of dreams in there and he felt he was waking to the cruel, cold, real world when he walked outside.

When they reached the warm classroom of the

95

Crime Academy, Smiff spread his note on a desk and
they read the message.

The wind is slight tonight little Ellen. . .
unlucky for some – so on until time halts. . .
Dream richly I value everything!

Now I am sure you have worked out exactly
what the message said. You can skip this page and
give yourself a large bar of chocolate as a reward.
But for the one reader in a hundred, the one who
is not quite as clever as a goose with no head,
here is what Smiff did with it next. He wrote the
words in a list:

The
wind
is
slight
tonight
little
Ellen
. . . unlucky for some

so
on
until
time
halts. . .

Dream
richly
I
value
everything!

"There we are," Dreep said. "Take the first letters of each word and it spells out the name and address you need to burgle tonight."

"Yes, I know that, I know that," Alice said crossly. "But what's that bit in the middle? Unlucky for some?"

Dreep and Smiff looked at one another and spoke together, "Number thirteen!"

"I knew that," Alice said with a scowl. "I just wondered if you scarecrow-heads had managed it. Well done."

"So-o," the boy nodded. "The victim is Twistle and the address is 13 South Drive. That's up the hill to the south, isn't it?"

"It is. Now Mayor Twistle is at the show. It won't finish till ten o'clock at the earliest and you'll be back here long before then. But, just to be on the safe side, George will send them a message inviting them to have dinner with him in the star dressing room . . . people like the Twistles will love that. They won't get home till eleven o'clock or even midnight. The constables are across the river so all you two need are your burglary kits!"

Smiff and Alice collected the bags of crowbars and skeleton keys, swag bags and dark lanterns. As they were about to leave there came a curious

and eerie whistle. "What was that?" Smiff squeaked.

He was getting nervous and that's why his voice squeaked. That's why mice squeak when they are chased by a cat. Nerves. You never hear a mouse shouting "You can't catch me, cat," in a deep voice, do you?

"A whistling wall!" Alice said. "I've never seen one of those before!"

Dreep chuckled. "It is a dumb waiter."

"Who says? You says? Doesn't sound very dumb to me!" Alice grumbled.

"When this building was a house THIS room was the dining room. The kitchens were down in the basement. The food was sent up in a little rope lift set in the wall." Dreep opened a small door in the wall.

"But what's the whistle?" Smiff asked.

"Someone below blows into a tube in the kitchen and there is a whistle in the other end of the tube up here in the dining room."

He took the paper and drew a quick sketch to show how it worked.

"Pull the whistle out at this end," Dreep explained,

doing just that. "Put your ear to the tube . . ." which
he did. ". . . and when someone speaks into the tube
below you can hear it up here! But first give them a
whistle to show you're ready."

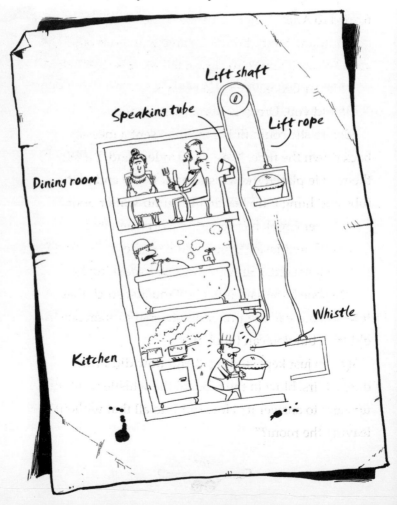

Dreep placed the tube to his mouth, blew and then spoke into it. "Hello!"

He placed it back to his ear and listened long and hard giving grunts and nods from time to time. Smiff turned to Alice, "There must be someone downstairs!

"Brilliant. Smiff, I'd never have worked it out," she said. "Now, if you're so clever, tell me who it is? Hah!"

"Master Crook!" Smiff shot back.

"I told you, Dreep is Master Crook and. . ."

Before she could finish the man sent a message back down the tube. "Yes, sir, I understand. I'll tell them." He placed the whistle back in the end of the tube and hung it up beside the dumb-waiter door.

"Master Crook has some . . . worrying news. . ."

"YOU are Master Crook," Alice sighed.

Dreep smiled. "So who was I just speaking to?"

"No one," she said quickly. "You just stuck that tube to your ear and pretended to chat to someone. An old trick but you can't fool me."

Dreep just kept smiling. "And how did I run downstairs, blow in the tube till the whistle went, run upstairs to answer it? How did I do all that without leaving the room?"

Alice looked furious. Her mouth moved but no words came for a while. Smiff had to hide a smile behind his hand. At last she said, "Yes, well, there's someone down in the basement. . ."

"Master Crook," Dreep said quietly. "And he has a message. It seems our friend and teacher, Bert the Burglar, has been arrested and locked up in the police station next door."

"Poor Bert!" Smiff cried. "Will he be all right?"

"Oh, yes," Dreep said. "He WILL be . . . because Master Crook says that after you've done the burglary you can break into the police station and set Bert free!"

"Can we?" Alice snapped. "Why should we?"

"Because," Smiff said, "we have to stick together. When it's your turn to get locked up then you know we'll all come and help to get you out. Isn't that right, Mr Dreep?"

"I will NOT get caught!" Alice raged.

"We all think that," Smiff shrugged. "But it could happen."

Of course, as he spoke, he didn't know just how soon his words would come true. It was almost as if he was the Spirit Master looking into the future – the very near future.

Chapter 7

SHOW SNOW

Constable Liddle and Constable Larch shivered. They hid in the bushes and looked across the snow-covered lawns of the hospital. "Why can't these burglars do their burgling on a nice sunny day?" Liddle grumbled. The snow was sliding inside his hard leather collar and making his neck sore.

Larch muttered, "If Inspector Beadle knows so much about this robbery then why isn't he out here?"

"Because it's snowing and cold and he's sitting back at the police station in front of a blazing fire," Liddle told him. "That boy that looked like the little match-girl that told us about the burglary.

I bet he's not shivering like us!"

But Liddle was wrong.

Alice wrapped her thin jacket tight around her thinner body and headed into the snow. The wind had now dropped and the snowflakes were huge and soft . . . just like on Christmas cards.

Except on Christmas cards they are painted on cardboard. They don't melt on your face and dribble cold water into your eyes. Christmas card flakes don't cling to your boots and trickle in at the ankles; they don't turn your nose blue. In fact the huge soft flakes were nothing like the ones on Christmas cards. I wish I hadn't said that. Forgive me.

The map that Samuel Dreep had drawn for her was getting wet. They climbed the hill towards the rich part of town. The front doors of these houses were at the end of sweeping drives for the carriages. Railings kept out stray dogs, fine trees inside the fences gave shelter from the winter snows or shade in the summer sun.

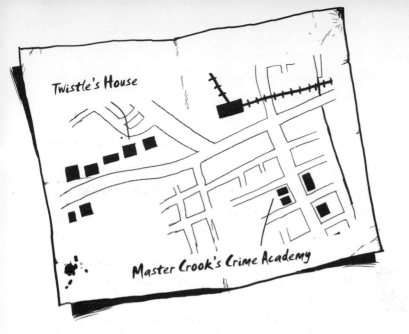

Twistle's House

Master Crook's Crime Academy

At last they reached South Drive. Alice turned to Smiff and reminded him, "Walk along the front, Bert the Burglar said. Get a feel for the way the house is laid out."

"But enter at the back where no one can walk past and see you," Smiff nodded. Their voices were muffled by the softness of the snow.

There was no one to see them in that wintry street. But carriage tracks showed that the people of South Drive could come past at any time. They slipped inside the shelter of number thirteen's gateway. The

high iron gates were open. They'd be closed after the Twistles came back from the music hall.

They looked up at the silent house. "The front door is in the middle so the stairs will be in the middle. When we get in you check the bedrooms to the right of the landing and I'll do the ones to the left," Alice said. "That's where the jewels will be – in the bedrooms."

Smiff nodded. "The show will be over soon. We'd better hurry. Just in case they don't go to dinner with George the Spirit Master. They may want to get home before the snow gets too deep."

"You aren't as stupid as you look, Smiff," Alice said sourly.

"You are as clever as you look," the boy told her then muttered, "Not very."

"Let's find the back lane," Alice said.

They ran down South Drive to the end, turned right then right again so they were in a dark, narrow lane that ran behind the houses. "How will we know which one is number thirteen?" Smiff asked. The wall that ran along the back was broken up with gates to the carriage houses as well as small doors. Some houses seemed to have two back doors. It made counting tricky.

There was no light in the lane but the snow gave the doors a glow and showed there were brass numbers nailed to the doors. "So the delivery men know where to go," Alice said pointing at one of the numbers.

They found number thirteen around the middle of the row. The back gate was bolted. There was broken glass set into the top of the wall to keep out burglars. But there was a gap between the top of the wooden door and the frame. A gap too narrow for burglars like Bert, but just wide enough for someone as bone-thin as Alice.

Smiff lifted her up, she grasped the top of the door and pushed her head through the gap. Then she wriggled her body through. Her legs followed and she managed to grab the door frame to stop herself shooting through and landing on her head. She pulled the bolt open. The gate stuck in the drift of snow but with Smiff pushing from the outside he opened it. He kicked away the pile of snow so the gate opened still wider. "What you doing?" Alice snapped. "You're in."

"But when we come out this way we'll have all the loot, won't we?" he explained. "We need it to open wide."

"Oh . . . yes . . . well, I knew that," Alice said and led the way up the back yard path to the rear of the Twistle house.

Half a dozen steps led up to the back door and half a dozen led down to a door in the basement. "Which door?" Smiff asked.

"The higher one if we want to get to the bedrooms."

Smiff trotted up, pulled out his skeleton key and tried to open it. "No use," he said. "There's a key on the inside of the lock."

"We can turn it and push it out. Bert showed us."

"I know, but it will take time. The basement might be easier."

Alice nodded. She led the way down the steps. She turned the handle of the door. She turned to Smiff. "It's open!"

The door led into a small corridor. Alice opened her leather bag and took out her lantern and matches. She lit the candle and closed the lantern front so just a narrow beam of light shone out. A solid oak door stood in front of them. Alice turned the door knob and felt the door move smoothly inwards. "This one's

open too!" she said and almost smiled.

"Great!" he grinned. "It's our lucky day!"

Of course, it never works like that, does it? A wise man once said, "If something looks too good to be true then it probably IS." And YOU can see what was wrong, can't you? A rich person would only leave the door to the house open if. . . ?

Bert the Burglar sat by the fire in the police station cell. He had unpicked the lock, wandered out and found some cheese and bread in the constables' room. He made himself a pot of tea and took it back to his cell to sit there in comfort. As the coal sizzled he shook his head. "I feel bad," he said to the fire. "I have burgled since I was a boy. I know everything. But I don't always remember what I know, do I? I mean, that's how I came to get caught last time, wasn't it? How did I come to get caught?"

The fire spluttered at him but didn't give a sensible answer. Bert scratched his head. "Let's see . . . I picked a posh house. I made sure the owners were out – just like those kids tonight. I did everything I told them to do. Checked it from the front . . . went round to the

back. Climbed over the back gate and went to the back door. Two back doors . . . the upper one leads straight into the dining room, the bottom one leads into the basement."

Bert held the poker in his hand and twisted it in the glowing coals as you would twist a door knob. "That's it! I remember now! The basement door was open. And if I had remembered I'd have known what that meant! A rich person would only leave the door to the house open if . . . oh, dear! Oh, dear. Oh-dear-oh-dear-oh-dear!"

Constable Larch felt as stiff as one of the branches on the bush he was hiding under. Yet suddenly he went stiffer. "Liddle!" he hissed. "Look! Someone coming out of the back door of the hospital."

"The burglar," Liddle said. "He must have sneaked in when you were asleep!"

"I was NOT asleep! I was just . . . just closed my eyes to keep my eyeballs warm."

"Look . . . he's walking across the lawn to that little hut."

Larch pulled out the plan that showed the hospital. Larch jabbed a finger. "That's us here. . ." he said.

"Ooooh! We look like bushes, don't we?" Liddle said.

"These are bushes," his partner sighed.

"I thought you said they was us?"

"No, no . . . these are the bushes we're hiding under."

Liddle grinned. "If we are under the bushes that explains why you can't see us on the plan!" he nodded happily and snow slipped off his tall hat.

Larch sighed. "That man has come out of the medicine dispensary," he said pointing at the plan. "Looks like he's gone into the toilet!"

"Ah, yes, well even a burglar has to go sometimes," Liddle said.

"So let's catch him!" Larch cried, jumping up. "Oooof! Me knees is stiff! Hurry before he's finished."

"Catch him with his pants down!" Liddle said. "That's not very fair, is it? I mean even a burglar has to have some private moments, doesn't he?"

But Larch wasn't listening. He slithered through the snow to the hut, waving his rattle. In his other hand he carried his truncheon and he used it to hammer on the toilet door. "I arrest you in the name of the law. Come quietly and you won't get hurt. Come out with your hands in the air!"

111

Liddle arrived just in time to see the door swing open. Light spilled from the hospital windows and lit the face of the man inside. A middle-aged man with thin hair stuck across his scalp to cover the bald patch. His face was a mask of terror. "What's wrong?" he asked.

"I said put up your hands!" Larch shouted fiercely.

The man raised his hands.

His trousers fell down.

"Pick up your trousers . . . and raise your hands."

The man tried to do both. It wasn't easy. "What have I done?"

"Stolen from the hospital."

"No I haven't!"

"Aha!" Liddle said. "We just watched you come out."

"I work there . . . but I needed a widdle. If wanting a widdle's a crime then it's a new one to me. I've never heard of that law before," the man moaned.

"We had a tip-off from a boy . . . who looked a lot like a girl dressed as a boy. A burglar is out to steal laudanum from the hospital," Larch growled.

"Ah, but I work in the dispensary," the man said. "We never use laudanum."

"You don't?"

"Your tip-off must have been wrong," the man moaned.

"Yes," Larch nodded. "We thought that, didn't we, Liddle?"

"No, Larch."

"Well, I thought it. But it is our duty to check out all reports – even the unlikely ones. Now, sir, we'll let you get back to work."

"But. . ."

"Come along, you don't want to hang around here getting cold and we have arrests to make back in the town . . . especially a girl dressed as a boy."

"But. . ."

"Your hospital is safe while Larch and Liddle are on patrol, sir. Back you go."

"But . . . but. . ."

"Run along now!"

"But I haven't had my widdle and I'm bursting!" the man cried.

"Ah . . . yes . . . we'll be getting along, sir. Hope we didn't scare you." Larch said and stretched out a hand to shake the man's hand.

The man shook hands . . . and his trousers fell down.

"Evenin' all!" Liddle and Larch said together as

they hurried back across the bridge to the south side of the river. They would be back at the station much earlier than anyone expected, of course.

Mayor Twistle beamed his best smile and Lady Twistle fluttered her fan. "Oh, Spirit Master, we would love to have dinner with you!" her ladyship said. "Maybe you can see into the future?"

"Yes," Mayor Twistle laughed. "Tell us which horse will win the horse race on the Springwell Fields next month? I could make a fortune!"

George the Spirit Master bowed his head gently. "Show me a list of the runners and I will do my best. Now supper is served in my dressing room if you would care to step backstage. . ."

But as the mayor and his wife sailed out of their theatre box, a worried man with a whip whispered into the mayor's ear. "Oh dear!" Mayor Twistle cried and turned to his wife with a pained face. "Ostler here says the snow is getting heavier. If we don't leave now then the horses will never be able to pull the carriage up the hill. We could be stuck half way."

"Gracious me!" Lady Twistle moaned and her fan

fluttered like a wasp's wing. "You can't expect me to walk, Oswald!"

"No dear."

"I was so looking forward to talking with the Spirit Master," she sighed. "And to eating," she said, drooling just a little.

Do you do that? When you are hungry and you think of food, does your mouth go wet enough to flood the floor? Take a tip from me . . . keep your mouth shut. Nobody loves a dribbler . . . unless it's a football player, of course.

"Don't worry, Cook will prepare us a meal as soon as we get home. Sorry, Spirit Master, some other time," the mayor said briskly as a servant helped him into his heavy coat.

George chewed his lip, anxious. Letting Mayor Twistle go home this early was dangerous. "It would be a disaster!" he said aloud.

"What would?" Lady Twistle gasped. "Can you see into the future? Can you see us having a coach crash in the snow?"

"Stay in the hotel next door!" George said.

Mayor Twistle stamped his foot. "We have no night-clothes with us, we have no servants, no clean shirt and collar for me in the morning. Nonsense to waste money on an hotel when we live just a mile away! Let's go!"

And before the Spirit Master could think of another story to stall them, they were out of the theatre and into the waiting coach. The mayor would be home much earlier than anyone expected.

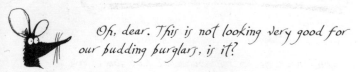

Oh, dear. This is not looking very good for our pudding burglars, is it?

Smiff opened the door into the basement room of 13 South Drive. Alice stood by his side.

They looked into the room where a fire burned by the kitchen stove and the heat melted the snow on their hats and clothes. Candles flickered in the draught from the door they had just opened.

Smiff's mouth went dry. He looked around the room. "Hello!" he said in a voice as weak as the water that dripped from his cap.

"Hello," Alice echoed.

Chapter 8

GREEN FIRE

You don't need me to tell you what had gone wrong, do you. You don't need me to tell you what Bert forgot to tell his jewel-snatching students.

You have already guessed, haven't you?

Smiff and Alice looked into the surprised faces of the Twistles' cook, the Twistles' butler, the Twistles' footman and the Twistles' maid-servant. "Good evening," the grey-faced, grey-haired butler said. "You must be burglars. Do come in and close the door. There's a terrible draught."

"Oh," Alice and Smiff said together.

"You see," Burglar Bert said to the fire, "there will be TWO back doors. The upper one will lead to the dining room in the house. The posh people can stroll out, after lunch, into the garden on sunny days. But there will be a second door to the basement. That's the one the servants use. They take in the deliveries. It leads to the kitchen. Now," he told an orange and purple flame. "Now . . . if the master and the mistress of the house are out the servants will not be in bed. They will be waiting to serve their master when he returns. They'll wait in the kitchen. So, whatever you do, do NOT go through the basement door."

The old man took the poker and stirred the fire. "That's the mistake I made. Ended up in prison for five years, didn't I?" The fire didn't reply. "I should have told my students that. Never mind, they may use a bit of common sense and work it out for themselves. They m-a-y get away with it." He shook his head. "I hope."

Constable Larch was warm and red-faced as he hurried over the town bridge. His chubby cheeks shone like apples . . . and not green apples. The sounds of the hammers and furnaces in the shipyard below were softened by the snow.

He had scribbled notes into his notebook. They were later printed up in the first Wildpool Police patrol report.

WILDPOOL POLICE FORCE

Constables Larch and Liddle proceeded to Wildpool Hospital and proceeded to hide under a bush. There they proceeded to observe the hospital and apprehended a suspicious character proceeding on his way to the little house at the bottom of the garden. Upon questioning the character he proved his innocence (he was in the act of proceeding to empty his bladder) so the officers proceeded back to the town centre where they suspected a crime was in the process of proceeding.

You will see I have found the report copied on to a Typographer machine. This is so you can read it more easily – and also because Constable Larch's nose dribbled on to the one he wrote in his notebook. It is quite disgusting – go and see it in Wildpool Museum if you don't believe me. Anyway, the speling was rubish.

The sparking lights and the workers' lanterns glowed bright then vanished behind another squall of snow. Larch was agitated. "You see, Liddle, what this means?"

"No, Larch."

"Someone sent us to the wrong side of town. We, the carriers of the truncheons of fire, are so fearsome they wanted us out of the way. They wanted us at the hospital while they burgled a house somewhere else!"

"Which house, Larch? There are only two thousand in Wildpool. What do you suggest? We search them all . . . a thousand each?"

"Aha! That is why we are policemen, Liddle. We are too clever for the cunning of the common criminal. We can out-think them, can't we?"

120

"Can we?"

"We can! For a start, if we were sent north of the river the robbery must be taking place to the south. Stands to reason. It will take place tonight . . . maybe at this very moment! And we know it won't be one of the houses by the riverside, will it?"

"Won't it?"

"No-o-o. They have nothing worth pinching, Liddle. No it will be one of the rich houses on the hill at the south end of the town."

"I think you're right – there's just a hundred of them! Fifty each. What do we do? Knock on the door and ask if they've seen any burglars in their bedrooms?" Liddle asked, struggling to keep up with his partner as they marched through the deep snow of the High Street. "Hang on, Larch, I'm not as young as I was."

"You're not as old as the river down there, but it runs a lot faster," Larch grumbled.

There were people pouring out of the theatre, laughing and chatting about the show they had just seen. Some pulled up their collars against the wind and others headed in happy groups towards the tavern.

Mayor Twistle's carriage creaked as it rolled out of the theatre's carriage-yard and on to the snow-covered road.

As the policemen reached the alley at the side of the Apollo music hall they skidded to a stop. A two-horse carriage was rumbling towards the main street and was not going to stop for anyone. The horses' nostrils smoked in the cold air as they strained to pull the carriage through the snow.

Larch held Liddle back so he wouldn't be trampled under hooves or crushed under wheels. "There should be a law against that!" Larch raged.

"Against what? Horses and carriages?"

"No. A law against speeding recklessly. A dangerous-driving law!"

"Hah!" Liddle chuckled. "That'll never happen!"

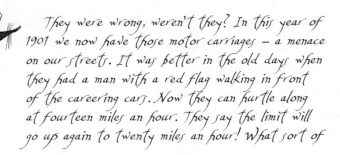

They were wrong, weren't they? In this year of 1901 we now have those motor carriages – a menace on our streets. It was better in the old days when they had a man with a red flag walking in front of the careering cars. Now they can hurtle along at fourteen miles an hour. They say the limit will go up again to twenty miles an hour! What sort of

madness is that? Someone will be killed if you ask me.

Suddenly a face appeared at the window. Not a very handsome face. The face was sat on the body of a gnome. "Halt!" the gnome cried to the carriage driver.

The driver pulled on the reins and pulled on the brake. The carriage slithered sideways and came to a halt. Mayor Twistle pushed his head out of the window and waved to the policemen. "You two!"

"Us, sir?"

"Yes . . . come over here and climb on the back of the carriage!"

Larch smiled happily and tugged at Liddle's sleeve to join him. "We'll get a lift all the way to the south hill," he told his partner. He put a foot on the back board of the carriage and hauled himself up. "You want us to sweep the streets of Wildpool clean of the filth that fouls its gutters, your honour?"

"No. I want you handy in case the coach gets stuck in the snow. You two can get off and push," Oswald Twistle snapped. "Home, James, and don't spare the horses!" he cried and slid up the window.

123

The driver raised his whip. "He loves shouting that . . . even if me name is Jack."

The carriage rolled over snow as white as Lady Arabella's face. It rolled out of the High Street and then the road began to climb the hill towards South Drive and the home of Mayor and Lady Twistle.

The almost-burgled home. . .

Alice was ready for this. She had pictured the scene in her mind. She threw herself into the act, more dramatic than the Wildpool Pantomime Players, more heart-breaking than Miss Nellie Sherrie (Sentimental vocalist, ballads and opera to bring tears to your eyes).

"Oh, I am undone. Oh, woe, woe, woe! The shame of my crime makes me wring my hands in grief. I know I am a poor and wicked girl. I know they will put the rope around my miserable neck and hang me from the gallows for all the world to see. And with my last breath I will say the words, 'I deserve it!' For I do. But who will pity me, miserable sinner that I am?"

She looked around the table. Four servant mouths hung open. Even Smiff was stunned. Alice's voice rose. "But if . . . if . . . you have one morsel of pity in

your hearts then hear my plea! I have walked down life's straight and crooked road and never barked up the wrong tree. Till tonight . . . when hunger drove me to this dreadful crime. Woe, woe. . ."

    "Whoa!" the grey-faced butler said, raising a hand. "Stop there, lass. We don't plan to turn you in."

    "What?"

    "No! We've been waiting years to meet someone like you. Come in, sit down and have a nice cup of

tea to warm you up," the cook said. She was a thin thing with hands as red as raw beef from washing and cleaning but her eyes were kind. Alice slid on to a seat beside her and wrapped her hands around a mug of tea. Smiff sat opposite.

"But we came to burgle you," Smiff said.

The footman was a handsome young man with a smooth face and a cheeky grin. "No you didn't."

"Sorry . . . we did!" Smiff argued.

The maid-servant was a lot bigger than Alice – quite a pale-faced pudding of a girl really; her shoulders were broad and strong but bent from carrying heavy trays, turning mattresses, carrying coal buckets, scrubbing floors, washing sheets and heaving heavy shopping up the hill to the house. She spoke softly. "You came to burgle Sir Bossy-Ossie Twistle, not us."

"If we thought we could get away with it we'd burgle him ourselves!" the butler said.

"You would?" Smiff smiled.

"Yes. But we need someone to do the deed and get away. We'd help, of course – show you where they keep all the best stuff. Give you the keys. . ."

"We can pick locks," Alice said.

"Ah, but that takes time. Much quicker if we just open up for you," the cook said.

"Why would you do that?" Smiff asked. "Is this a trick?"

"No trick," the footman said. "But if Nancy were to roll up her sleeves you'd see the bruises where Lady Twistle beat her," he went on, nodding to the maid-servant.

"And I can show you the housekeeping books where if anything is broken the money comes out of our wages," the butler went on. He nodded towards the cook. "Elsie there broke a cup in the washing up. Lady lemon-face Twistle said it was part of a precious set and would cost Elsie a pound in wages."

The cook sighed. "That's a month's wages. And they even make us pay for the food we eat and the tea we drink."

Alice felt the warmth of the fire and the warmth of her temper turning her face red. "So why don't you leave?"

The butler shook his head. "The Twistles would make sure no one else would give us a job. We'd end in the poorhouse. This life is bad but the poorhouse is worse."

"Look. Here is what they ate at their Christmas dinner party they had," the butler said taking a sheet of paper and showing it to the burglar guests.

**MONEY TALKS
Gold talks loudest!**

MENU

SOUPS
Pheasant soup or clear soup
Sherry wine

FISH
Turbot with tartare sauce
Hock wine

ENTREES
Lobster cream or mashed wild duck
Champagne wine

ROAST
Saddle of mutton or partridges
Claret wine

SWEETS
Pine~apple fritters or Noyeau Cream
Madeira wine

ICES
Maraschino and brandy liqeurs

CHEESE
Stilton
Port wine

VEGETABLES WITH JOINT
Potatoes & Spinach, green peas

"We get to eat the leftovers," the cook said, "so it's not all bad, is it, Maurice?" she asked the footman. He shook his head.

"So," the footman went on with the story, "we have to get our revenge in any way we can. Some of the things Cook slips into their soup . . . well, you wouldn't want to know."

I am sure, nosey reader, you WOULD want to know. But you will just have to guess. I will just say this. If you ever go to a restaurant to eat, never say anything nasty to the chef. His revenge can be rotten . . . and so can your food.

"But we always hoped one day someone would come along and give them a good burgling. And here you are!" the cook cried.

The servants stood up and busied themselves. "Silver knives and forks on a silver serving tray," the butler said. He spread them on the tablecloth and bundled them up. "There you are, son," he said turning to Smiff. "What's your name . . . no . . . better if you don't tell me."

"But the police will suspect you!" Smiff cried.

"No . . . we'll unlock the upper back door and make it look as if you came in that way while we were all down here in the basement. Don't worry," the butler said. "We've spent many a happy hour talking about this. Planning it. Come on . . . time to head upstairs. There are a few tasty pieces of jewellery that'll make a pretty penny."

"Can't we share them with you?" Smiff asked.

"Better not," the maid-servant Nancy said as she led the way through the dimly lit hall to the stairs. "If we suddenly start to look rich someone will notice."

Maurice the footman shrugged. "We just want to see the looks on their greedy little faces – that will be payment enough for us," he said. And so they started to gather some of the jewels from Lady Twistle's dressing table and slip them into the sack Alice had brought with them.

"Of course Lady Twistle likes to buy a lot of flashy jewellery that's no better than glass," the maid-servant Nancy said. "But I can show you the really valuable pieces – the ones her rich mother left in her will. There are some emeralds that would be fit for Princess Victoria herself! And please take this solid silver

hairbrush . . . it's the one she beats me with."

Nancy opened a drawer and showed Alice the great gems that shone with a green fire of their own. Alice's eyes were wide with wonder. It was almost a pity to hide their beauty in her dusty bag.

"This is so-o easy," Smiff said.

But remember what I said about things that are too good to be true. . .

Inside the carriage, the white-faced, pink-cheeked, red-lipped, wig-headed, fan-waving Lady Twistle suddenly called out, "Can't we hurry, Oswald?"

"Why is that, my buttercup?" he asked.

"The Spirit Master has taught me so much tonight . . . I can feel his power in me!" she said and her voice trembled - or it may have been her stomach rumbling with hunger. "I have a bad feeling!"

"A few glasses of champagne will settle you, my dear," he said and patted her knee.

"There is something wrong at the house. I know it, Oswald, I know it. Hurry!"

The mayor sighed but lowered the window. "Home,

James and don't spare the horses!"

"I'm going as fast as I can," the driver, Jack, called down from his seat.

"Then it is not fast enough! Get those chaps at the back to push!" Mayor Twistle ordered.

The policemen jumped down and put their backs to the coach. Their boots skidded and they spent as much time falling on their rattles and truncheons and handcuffs as they did pushing. But at last they reached the top of the hill and the end of South Drive.

The horses steamed and snorted like fire-breathing dragons and padded along the drive.

They turned in at the front gates.

If it hadn't been snowing they would have seen that the front door was opening and two small thieves, loaded down with loot, were stepping out.

Chapter 9

SHIP OF SAFETY

Nancy the maid looked down the front drive and was the first to see the carriage lights, glowing in the snowy air. "It's the master!" she cried. "Run!"

"Which way?" Alice shouted into the wind. "No use telling us to run like headless gooses."

"Out the basement door!" the butler said.

Alice was holding the front handle of the solid-silver serving tray and Smiff was holding the back. The loot was piled on top of it. It was clumsy to carry but the burglars had come too far to let go now. They clattered through the house and into the kitchen. They had just reached the basement door

133

as Mayor Twistle reached the front door.

Two frozen, white-coated policeman looked down from the back of the coach.

Yes, I know they had been navy blue-coated, but they looked more like plaster statues, white and solid, after riding a mile as coachmen.

The mayor had jumped down from the carriage before his driver could open the door for him. He half-dragged his wife from the carriage as she squawked, "Don't be so clumsy, Ossie!"

Mayor Twistle trotted up the steps to where the butler stood by the door. "What's wrong?" he demanded.

The butler twisted his grey hands together in misery. "Oh, Sir Oswald, Sir Oswald, we been robbed!"

"We can't have been!" Lady Arabella Twistle exploded.

I don't mean she actually exploded, of course. That would have left bits of silk dress and fat

134

*splattered on the mat. There is nothing so
disgusting as a fat-splattered mat. No. Her
words exploded.*

"No one would dare to rob the greatest lady in
Wildpool!"

"And the greatest man," the mayor chipped in.

"We was all in the kitchen having a little dried
bread and dripping for supper," the butler said. "Then
Cook thought she heard a sound – a door slam in one
of the bedrooms!"

"My jewels!" Lady Twistle screamed and rushed
through the hall and up the stairs, fast as a ferret up a
drainpipe.

"How did they get in?" Twistle demanded.

"Through the front door while we were in the
back?" the butler suggested.

At that moment Constables Larch and Liddle
walked stiffly up to the door. "Aha!" Larch said.
"There would be footprints in the snow if they had
come in this way!"

"Well done, Constable!" the mayor cried.

"Ah!" the butler said and he gulped like a frog

swallowing a fat bee. You can see his problem. If the thieves didn't come in through the front door then they must have come through the basement door . . . and the servants must have seen them . . . which they did! It was b-i-g trouble for butler, cook, footman and maid.

But Nancy the moon-faced maid was standing in the shadow of the staircase and heard the policeman. She thought quickly. She pulled the footman towards the dining room at the back of the house. "The dining room door to the garden has to be open!" she said to him. She unlocked the door then threw the key on to the floor. It looked as if burglars had pushed the key out and used a skeleton key.

"Now we need footprints running away from this door, over the snow to the back gate . . . then footprints back into the house! Quick!"

The two ran over to the back gate – it was unbolted where Smiff and Alice had just run out.

"Good," Nancy cried. "Now, back into the house!"

They ran back to the dining room door and were in the hallway just in time to bow to the mayor as he and Constable Larch marched through. As Larch said:

WILDPOOL POLICE FORCE

REPORT

Constables Larch and Liddle proceeded through the house to the dining room. The door into the garden was open. Footsteps came into the room and footsteps ran away to the back gate. This was clearly the means by which the burglarizing villains had gained entry. I was about to search the garden for other clues when Lady Twistle entered the room and described the loss of her valuables. The lady was in a very agitated state. She did not speak polite enough for a police report. But she said. "The _____ _____ have nicked me best _____ jewels and the _____ have left the cheap _____ glass stuff behind. I want the _____ caught and I want the _____ tortured till they beg to be _____ hanged and I will put the rope round their miserable _____ necks myself!" Then the butler pointed out that the solid silver tray with the silver knives and forks had gone from the dining room. Mayor Twistle was upset. His language was even worse than his wife's. He sort of said. "Oh, dear. they cost a lot of money. I do hope the criminals will be caught and punished very harshly."

Mayor Twistle also complained that the constables were dripping melted snow on to his expensive carpet and the bill would be sent to Inspector Beadle.

Constables Larch and Liddle then proceeded to the front door with Mayor Twistle to report the theft at the police station.

The constables were asked to ride outside of the coach so they did not drip on to the expensive leather seats of the coach.

The coach turned in the drive and rumbled back towards the road at South Drive. It turned slowly. If only the driver had been faster at turning. If only the horses hadn't been so cold and scared of slipping. If only the driver hadn't dropped the whip from his frozen fingers.

If the coach had rolled into South Drive a minute earlier . . . the policemen would have seen two small figures scurrying along, carrying a silver tray between them piled with a bundle of clanking loot. For Alice and Smiff had struggled down the back lane of the houses, through the ever-deeper snow and on to the front of South Drive. There they could trot through the carriage tracks and go much faster. But of course they could be seen by any passing pigeon or postillion.

Now we have these petrol cars you don't see so many carriages. You young people may not even know what a postillion does! He sits on one of the carriage horses and uses it to guide the others. You could always tell a postillion by his horsey smell. Very smelly things – sweaty horses, but not as smelly as those smoky petrol cars!

But the coach was slow. It had to drive around drifts and then it began to slide sideways when it reached the hill down to the High Street. The driver was half-blinded by the snow.

It meant that Alice and Smiff reached the Crime Academy before the coach arrived at the police station next door.

The burglars' faces were glowing as they raced into the classroom and placed the silver tray on the classroom desk.

Samuel Dreep had a warm fire blazing for them and rubbed his twig fingers in glee. "Ah! I can see we

have two star academy pupils here. Well done!"

"We were almost caught!" Alice panted. "Barmy old Bert forgot to tell us about the two doors at the back of the house."

Dreep nodded. "Yes, you are so right, Alice. It is time Bert retired. He should go and live with his sister at her little cottage in the country. He's been caught once. If he's caught again it could be the gallows for him. Yes, he's lived a hard life and his last years should be spent in peace."

"Leave burglary to young ones like me and Alice?" Smiff said.

"Exactly!" Dreep chuckled. "That's what Master Crook's Crime Academy is all about."

"So why doesn't Bert just go?" Alice said angrily. "Save us getting caught with his awful advice?"

Dreep shook his head. "Bert's sister is poor as a church mouse, Alice. She can't afford to feed herself let alone her burglar brother. No, Bert needs to take enough cash with him so they can live together in comfort."

"We can give him some of this loot!" Smiff said.

"I hoped you'd say that," Dreep smiled. He

untied the bundle and looked at the loot. He divided it into two piles and wrote down what was there.

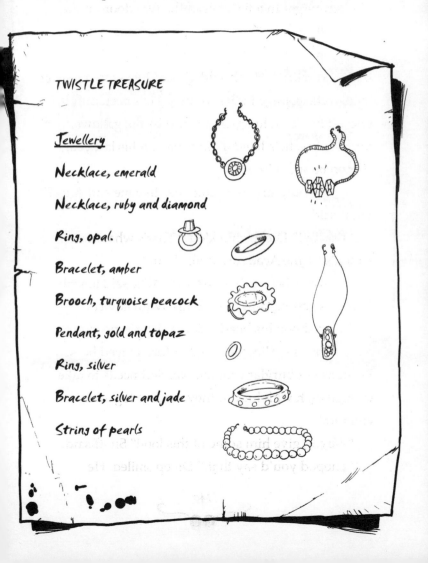

TWISTLE TREASURE

<u>Jewellery</u>

Necklace, emerald

Necklace, ruby and diamond

Ring, opal.

Bracelet, amber

Brooch, turquoise peacock

Pendant, gold and topaz

Ring, silver

Bracelet, silver and jade

String of pearls

<u>72-piece Fiddle, Thread & Shell Cutlery Set.</u>

Dinner knives, sterling silver, 12

Dinner forks, 12

Dessert forks, 12

Dessert knives, 12

Soup spoons, 12

Tea spoons, 12

<u>Extra</u>

Solid silver serving tray – oval, sterling silver,

3 foot wide, ivory handles

"Now, Master Crook has left instructions. He wants half of the winnings to be sold so you two can live a little better – warmer clothes and better food for your families."

"I'm going to buy a brand new mop bucket for my mother!" Smiff said. "She can never have too many mop buckets."

Dreep placed the jewels in his pocket. "I'll take these out of town and sell them for cash." He wrapped the silver knives and forks in the cloth again and tied them. "Now, Master Crook wants you to put these somewhere where the police can find them."

"What! Who says? You says?" Alice cried. "We go to all that risk to steal them and crazy, creepy Crook wants us to give them back? Here . . . let me have a word with him!" She stomped over to the dumb waiter message tube and blew down it. When a low voice answered at the other end she shouted, "Here! What's this about giving our stealings back?" She placed the tube to her ear and listened. "Yeah, but . . . no . . . I see . . . oh . . . we-ell . . . I suppose."

She hung up the speaking tube and turned to Smiff. "There's this new police force in Wildpool," she said.

Smiff just nodded.

"Well, they are not very good . . . and that suits us."

"True!"

"So-o Master Crook says we have to make them

look good," Alice went on.

Smiff's eyes went bright. "Great idea! If they fail in this first great crime they'll get the sack . . . Wildpool could get some good policemen and we'd be finished! That's why Master Crook is such a master! He thinks ahead."

"So," Dreep said. "That's agreed." He sat at the desk and looked at the wet burglars. "Now, you have had a tough day's work . . . and I'm sorry, but you're not finished yet."

Alice blew out her cheeks and tried to hold in her anger. "We have to set Bert free, don't we?"

"That was part of your task for tonight," Dreep nodded and spread his fine fingers, helpless. "Sorry."

Smiff shrugged. "I suppose we could give him his solid silver tray, and take the knives and forks to dump where the police will find them?"

"Hang on!" Alice raged. "Bert can't escape in this weather! He can't walk off to see his sister when the roads are choked with snow. It's bad in the town . . . it'll be worse in the country. He'll be dead before morning!"

"Suppose so," Smiff sighed.

144

"No," Dreep told them, his green eyes twinkling in the firelight. "Bert can head down Low Street to the docks. There's a coal ship leaves on the midnight tide. It'll drop him off down south, he'll get cash for the tray . . . it's all arranged. Set Bert free then get him down to the quayside. Easy."

Nothing is ever easy in the world of crime, as you have learned. And you, dear reader, can see what is going to happen, can't you? Of course you can! But can you see the way our heroes will get away? Or can you see them swinging on the end of a rope – or worse?

What's worse than swinging on the end of a rope? you ask. Well, being put in a gibbet was worse. You don't see them about these days. But back in 1837 it wasn't enough to execute a criminal. Some of them were taken down after they were dead. Their corpses were painted all over with tar so they didn't rot. Then they were put in a metal cage. The cage was hung up at the roadside so everyone could see them.

There was a famous one at Attercliffe, you may have heard about? It was so very popular and the body didn't rot for forty years!

AWESOME ATTERCLIFFE

THE PERFECT PLACE FOR YOUR PICNIC
TAKE THE TRAIN TO THIS SUNNY SPOT AND
HAVE A GREAT FAMILY DAY OUT

DAY RETURNS FROM WILDPOOL ONE SHILLING
PER ADULT – THIRD CLASS
CHILDREN UNDER FIVE TRAVEL FREE!
A GREAT DAY OUT YOU'LL NEVER FORGET

LNER Railway Company Limited

"The police are up at the Twistle house," Smiff said. "I suppose this is the best time to go and set Bert free?"

"What about Inspector Beadle?" Alice asked.

Dreep smiled. "He'll be snug and warm in his basement, writing reports for the mayor. Don't worry about him!"

Alice and Smiff picked up the tray with the silverware and carried it back into the snow. The front door to the police station was open and a gas lamp sizzled softly in the entrance hall. A helpful sign said:

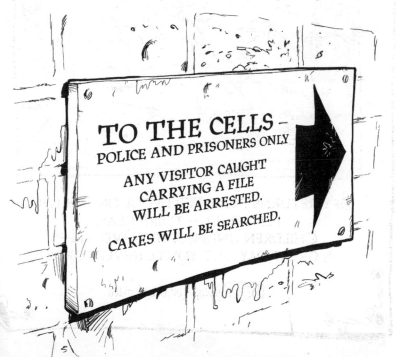

TO THE CELLS –
POLICE AND PRISONERS ONLY

ANY VISITOR CAUGHT
CARRYING A FILE
WILL BE ARRESTED.

CAKES WILL BE SEARCHED.

"Why would they search a cake?" Smiff asked.

"Because, you dummy, friends take a cake to the prisoner and slip a file inside," Alice said.

"In case they fancy doing a bit of woodwork?"

"No – to file through the bars," Alice said growing more angry.

"We haven't brought a file!"

"No, worm-brain, because we can pick locks."

Smiff smiled. "So can Bert."

"True," Alice said shortly.

Of course Alice was a short girl. Anything she said would be short. A bit like Mayor Twistle and every one of Snow White's dwarfs. But if you say something "shortly" it means you are a little grumpy. Exactly like ONE of Snow White's dwarfs.

And when they walked down the passage to the cell they saw the door swinging open. Bert sat inside, poking the small fire. He looked up and frowned. "Oh, there you are! Am I pleased to see you! I was so worried cos I forgot to tell you something in this morning's lesson. . ."

"Too right you did, you old goat!" Alice raged. "You forgot—"

"It all worked out fine in the end," Smiff cut in. "This silver tray is your part of the loot."

The old man smiled happily. "Well done, my star students!" he said.

"Why haven't you escaped?" Alice asked.

Bert frowned. "It's cold out there! I thought I'd stay here snug and warm till the weather turned a bit better," he explained.

"There's a ship waiting to take you to the port near where your sister lives," Smiff said. "Safer if you leave now. Come on!"

"Safer?" Bert asked. "Why?"

Smiff shook his head. "I don't know why I said that . . . I just have a bad feeling. We shouldn't be in a police station half an hour after we've done a robbery."

"Right!" Bert said. "Let's go before those constables get back."

And so the three burglars slipped quietly into the corridor and walked quickly to the front door of the police station.

They opened it just as a carriage turned into the High Street.

Mayor Twistle opened the carriage door and looked down from the top step. "Bert the Burglar!" he cried. "THAT'S the man that burgled my house! Arrest that man! This time he'll hang for sure!"

"We had him locked away, sir," Liddle said from his step at the back.

"Well he escaped, you buffoon. You can SEE he's escaped. But he won't escape again! Not with Sir Oswald Twistle on the case. Forward, James, and don't spare the horses!"

Jack cracked his whip.

Chapter 10

TRAY AWAY

The carriage was dragged past the police station, past Master Crook's Crime Academy at the pace of a greyhound . . . a sleeping greyhound. Smiff's granny could have moved faster and, as you know, she was long dead and on the dung heap. The snow was deep and the whole town seemed silent.

It would have been quicker to walk – the long-legged policemen would have caught the young burglars and their limping old teacher. But Mayor Twistle did not want to wet his fine boots more than he had to.

"On James! Don't spare the horses!"

Jack turned and shouted back, "Maybe if the

policemen got out and pushed it would help?"

"Good idea! Liddle! Larch! Off and push!" Twistle roared. "I'll teach Wildpool criminals that it doesn't pay to tangle with a Twistle."

The constables jumped down. The coach moved a little faster . . . but still a lot slower than the policemen if they hadn't had a coach to push. They slithered along, sweat running down under their helmets and stinging their eyes.

The High Street was high above the river.

Maybe that's why it was called the High Street. Of course in the heat of summer, when the fly-crusted horse droppings and the sewage-blocked drains made the place stink then some people say it smelled "high". High or high, you decide why.

The workers had given up clanging hammers on the new railway bridge over the river. The workers at the new railway station had come down from the iron roof now. It was too slippery and cold to hold on to the scaffolding.

In the docks the coal was loaded on to the ships waiting for the tide to carry them out into the sea. The gas lights glittered in the streets and Wildpool almost looked pretty in its white blanket.

Alice heard the mayor calling out in the soft, white silence, and shouted, "Hurry, Bert! They'll catch you long before you get down to the quayside."

"If I go any faster me legs'll drop off," Bert groaned. "I'm not as young as you!"

"You're not as young as most of the bones in Wildpool graveyard . . . but you'll be just as dead if you don't hurry up!" she urged.

The old man struggled on till he reached the top of Low Street. The steep street ran down to the river. There was a sharp bend at the bottom end of the road that led to the shipyards. But it was too far for Bert to struggle down the hill.

The carriage was closer now and at last Mayor Twistle saw what was plain as a snowfield. "Stop pushing, you pot-headed policemen! Run after them! You'll easily catch them." He climbed out of the door and worked his way alongside the driver who was panting with tiredness after a mile of whip-waving and rein-slapping.

The police pulled their weary legs through the

snow that was now up to their knees and headed towards the burglars at the top of Low Street.

For a moment Alice, Smiff and Bert looked back in horror at the navy-clad nasties coming closer and closer.

"Save yourselves," Bert gasped. "You youngsters . . . don't worry about me. I'll put up a fight. Make sure you get away. Go on! Push off!" he cried like a hero.

The police were twenty paces away now. Mayor Twistle looked on and cheered. "Forward, my brave lads! People of Wildpool! I wish they could see this glorious moment, James."

"We could tell the local paper," Jack suggested.

"No, no! I don't want anyone to know that I was the victim of this crime . . . they may laugh. And anyway, I don't want people to know that I have anything worth stealing! Next thing you know they'll be asking me for money to give to the poor in the poorhouse!"

Fifteen paces away now, Smiff's brain was racing like a greyhound.

Mayor Twistle was jumping up and down with such excitement the coach bounced on its springs. "Men in uniform will patrol the streets and guard our persons, guard our homes, guard our factories and

guard our wealth!" he sang happily without his wife's notes to help.

Ten paces . . . then Smiff made his move. "Give me the tray, Alice!" he ordered.

Alice was about to argue but saw the fierce joy in the boy's eyes and let go of her end. Smiff dropped it on to the snow and it sat there shining. He handed the bundle of silver knives and forks to Bert the Burglar. "Drop those off on your way down to the ship!" he said quickly.

"How do I get to the ship?" Bert asked.

"On a sledge," Smiff laughed. "Climb on the tray!"

Bert stepped on to the large silver tray and sat down clutching the silverware. "Ready, Alice?" Smiff asked.

With the policemen just five paces away the young burglars put their hands on the back of the tray and pushed. Slowly it slid down the steep hill of Low Street. When the police were three paces away it picked up speed.

"Whee!" Bert cried in glee. "It's like when I was a kid!"

The snow sprayed away. The policemen stopped to watch the old man vanish downhill, speeding ever faster past lampposts and doors. When he was a small

155

figure at the bottom of the hill he dropped the loot over the side, grasped the front of the tray, leaned to his left and guided the sledging tray round the sharp bend.

"He's escaped!" Mayor Twistle screamed! "Escaped with the loot! I can just see the headlines now . . . oh, how they'll laugh!"

Sure enough the headlines in the paper the next day were not kind to Twistle and his new police force.

THE WILDPOOL STAR

5 January 1837

SNOW HOPE OF CATCHING TWISTLE THIEVES

Thieves raided the home of Wildpool Mayor, Sir Oswald Twistle, during a snowstorm and skated away with some of the Twistle treasure!

Witness Jack Ostler (who does not wish to be named) said, "The old burglar just jumped on a tray and sledged away. The kids that were with him ran off down Low Street and vanished into a house. It was quite funny really!"

Liddle and Larch stopped to watch the speeding man and that gave Alice and Smiff the chance to run and slither down the hill and into Smiff's front door before the constables could catch them.

But Master Crook's cunning plan was not complete, of course. Twistle had seen the cloth dumped at the bottom of the hill and cried, "My valuables! I can get my valuables! Down the hill, James, and don't spare the horses."

Jack turned and said, "Sorry, sir, but we probably couldn't get the coach down that hill without crashing – it's far too steep. And it's stone certain we wouldn't get back up again."

Twistle clenched his hands into fists of fury and beat them against the roof of the carriage. "Liddle!" he shouted. "Go down the hill and fetch my treasure."

"I'll have to dig through those snowdrifts . . . it could be anywhere. Can't we wait till it thaws?"

"Wait? Wait? What if some villains come along and find it first? Do you think they will trot up to South Drive and hand it back to me?"

"They would if they were honest," Liddle argued.

The mayor's eyes were bulging and his face red

as a radish as he screamed, "If they were honest they wouldn't be villains, you clown of a constable!"

"That's true, sir."

"As for you, Larch, I want you to arrest Bert the Burglar's accomplices," the mayor went on. "If we can't hang Bert in front of the town jail then we can hang them."

"We don't know if they were there at the scene of the crime," Larch argued.

"It doesn't matter, Constable Clod. I will say I saw them . . . my servants will say they saw them. I want someone hanged."

"Even if they're innocent?"

"Yes . . . even if they're innocent! I will not be laughed at by the people of Wildpool. Now check those houses – find out which one they ran into – arrest them and lock them up . . . and tie them up so they can't unpick your lousy locks."

"Yes, sir," Larch sighed and began to walk carefully down the steep and snowy street. He followed in the footsteps of Liddle who was half way to the bottom. Larch pulled out his truncheon and used it to knock on doors. The owners of the houses were not pleased.

"Do you know what time it is?" a woman asked.

"Time you had a clock," Larch snapped.

"I was getting my beauty sleep!" she said.

"It wasn't working very well," he said, shining his lantern into her pale face. "I am looking for a couple of boys," he said.

"Try the orphanage," she said.

"Two burglars who ran down here and entered one of these houses. Do you have two boys in the house?"

"No I do not. I have one girl and a very large husband who will not be pleased if I wake him up. Now let me get back to bed. It's freezing."

And so he made his slow way down the hill, one house at a time.

Constable Larch was being watched. He was being watched by Mayor Twistle from the top of the hill and by three people from a door in a house half way down the hill. . .

Mrs Smith peered around the door. "He's five doors away, Smiff. Chubby feller . . . big truncheon. Trouble is you couldn't get enough speed to run past him. One swish of that stick and he'd snap your legs. If

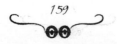

159

you think it's hard running in snow you should try running in snow with two broken legs! Cor! That would be a sight to see."

"Thanks, Mum," Smiff muttered.

"And of course you can't run down the hill cos that other policeman is at the bottom. The one with the droopy white moustache. Oh, yes! Looks impossible!"

Alice stood behind her in the hallway holding a small stump of candle. "Mrs Smith, if that's all you can say then I think I would prefer it if you shut up!"

"Ooooh! Get madam snappy-knickers," she laughed. "I said it looks impossible . . . but the Smith family have been in tighter corners than this and we're still around."

"So, what do you suggest?" Alice asked.

"Mop buckets!" Mrs Smith cackled.

"Mop buckets? Do you have one?"

"One? I've more than one. You can never have too many mop buckets, my dear," the woman said. "Go and get the one from the back kitchen – the one full of cold soapy water – I used it this afternoon to wash the kitchen floor."

Alice scowled but did as she was told. She brought

the sloshing bucket to the door. Mrs Smith said, "Good girl. Now watch this!" She opened the door and threw the cold water on to the pavement, just down the hill from her door. Then she closed the door and took the candle into the small living room. The fire had burned out and the ashes were cold now . . . but not as cold as the water on the pavement. That had melted the snow outside and begun to turn into a beautiful sheet of ice.

Two minutes passed. There was a sharp rap at the door from a police truncheon.

Mrs Smith clapped her hands softly and said, "Now, watch this . . . see how a mop bucket can save your life!"

She walked towards the shabby door. Alice and Smiff crept into the hallway and hid behind the door as Mrs Smith pulled it open. "Ooooh! Good evening, constable! I have heard all about you and your partner."

"You have?"

"Well . . . not ALL. I mean, they didn't tell me how handsome you were. I love a man in uniform."

"Yes, well. . ."

"My husband looked smart in his uniform," Mrs Smith said and gave a giggle.

"Was he a policeman?"

"No he was in the prison service," Mrs Smith said, and all the time she kept Larch talking the ice grew harder and the snow was covering the slippery patch.

"Ah, your husband was a prison warder then?"

"No – he was a prisoner at Darlham Gaol. But he did look lovely in that prison uniform. Not as lovely as you though, handsome!"

"Yes, madam . . . now, I am looking for a couple of boys!"

"Me too!" Mrs Smith screamed in delight.

"What?"

"A couple of nice handsome boys to cuddle me . . . it gets so cold at night, doesn't it? You and your partner are the answer to a maiden's dreams!"

"Madam," Larch said, alarmed, "I am looking for two burglars. They were seen to enter a property on this side of the street. Have you seen them?"

"Oh, those two? Yes! I can show you where they went!" she said and stepped out on to the snowy pavement. "Take two steps down the hill . . . that's right," she went on, guiding him on to the slippery trap she'd laid.

"See? At the bottom of the hill? Searching through the snowdrift?"

"That's Police Constable Liddle!" he said.

"Yes, and you are going to join him!" she laughed. She placed a hand firmly in his back and pushed.

The man's boots scrabbled on the ice patch. They shot forward and into the air. He landed on his plump backside and by then was travelling so fast he ploughed through the snow like a hot knife through dripping.

He stretched out his arms to try to stop himself but it was no use. He sped like a shooting star down the steep hill and then the most amazing thing happened.

He stopped.

Of course you knew he would. He had to stop some time, didn't he? So what is amazing about that? you sneer. You shouldn't sneer. It makes you look ugly. And, as Smiff's granny used to say, "If the wind changes your face could stay like that." Ugh! Not a pleasant sight.

Chapter 11

CURTAIN OF CROOK

PC Larch stopped with a clatter. A tinkle of silver wrapped in a cloth.

"You found it!" PC Liddle cried. "You found the Twistle treasure! Well done, Larch."

"Ooooh! Me bum!" Larch groaned.

"What's wrong with it?"

"There's something sticking in it."

"Ah, yes, it's a fork. Hang on and I'll pull it out. . ."

"Careful. . . Aaaarrrrgh! Ooooh! That hurt," Larch sobbed.

"Wrap a bandage round it," Liddle shrugged.

Larch struggled to his feet. "The mayor will

be pleased," he said.

"The burglar got away," Liddle reminded him. "Sir Oswald was keen to have someone hanged outside the jail. Did you find the boys that were with Bert the Burglar?"

"I think so. I met a very odd woman . . . mad as a three-legged duck . . . but I think she was hiding someone."

"What number house was it?" Liddle asked.

"I forget now . . . I went to half a dozen houses. I guess we'll have to work our way back up the street," Larch sighed.

"It won't be easy getting up the hill . . . not as easy as coming down it."

"Easy? You call a slide that ends with a fork in your bum an 'easy' way to travel?" Larch snapped.

"Sorry," Liddle muttered and picked up the bag of loot. The policemen began to climb the hill but it was slow work. They slipped in the deep snow and clung to the walls of the houses to stay on their feet.

In the Smith house they were just waiting for the police to return, arrest them and hang them. . .

*

"Well done, Mum," Smiff sighed. "You got rid of the policeman for now, but he'll be back. There are two of them coming up the hill to get us."

"The mayor and his coachman are waiting at the top of the hill if we go that way," Alice put in. "We're trapped."

Mrs Smith shook her head. "Lor! I never met such a gloomy twosome. Remember what Granny used to say."

"Granny said a lot of things," Smiff said angrily. "Then she died and she isn't saying them any more."

Mrs Smith smiled calmly. "Granny always said 'It's not over till it's over'."

"Uh?" Smiff grunted.

But Alice nodded. "Wise words."

"What are you two on about?" Smiff groaned.

Alice's spark was burning again, as bright as the matches she used to sell. "We thought it was all over for Bert . . . but we sent him down the hill on that silver tray and he's free."

"We don't have any more silver trays," Smiff spat.

"No," his mother said cheerfully, "but we have something better. Something that will get you up the

hill to the only safe place – Master Crook's Crime Academy."

Smiff frowned. "The police are on their way up the hill. They may be slow but we're slower. . . Our legs are just too short to get through this snow. The mayor and the coachman will stop us if we get to the top."

"Not if you move too quickly to be caught, the way Bert did."

"Bert had a sort of sledge. We can't sledge up a hill!"

Mrs Smith nodded. "There is a place far, far to the north of here. . ."

"Scotland?" Smiff said.

"Even further than Scotland," his mother said. "And it is snow there all the time."

"Impossible," Smiff scoffed. "They couldn't grow food. What do they eat?"

"Fish."

"Is this another one of your stories, Mum?"

"No. This is something your father told me. He didn't always sail on coal ships you know. Sometimes he sailed up north through seas full of mountains they called icebergs. Look!"

She pointed to a map of the north that was pinned to the wall over the fireplace.

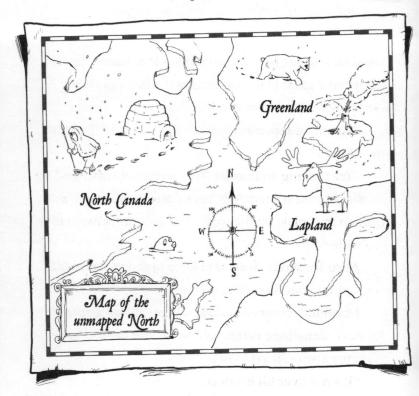

Greenland

North Canada

N
NW NE
W E
SW SE
S

Lapland

Map of the
unmapped North

"And that's where he met people who live in snow all the year round. Even their houses are made out of ice bricks.

Mrs Smith was telling the truth for once. These ice houses, or igloos, are great. Build one yourself and see next winter. Just don't have a house-warming party.

And he told me how these people get around . . . they wear great plates on their feet. They call them snowshoes. They don't sink into the snow . . . they walk over the top of it. "

"Plates?"

"Try floating an iron nail in a bucket of water and it sinks because it's narrow," his mother explained. "But put an iron plate on the water and it floats because it's so wide."

Alice scowled. "You want us to fasten plates to our feet and go out there?"

Mrs Smith beamed a smile wider than any plate. "I have something better," she said. "Remember what Granny always used to say?"

"It's not over till it's over?"

"No, the other thing she used to say – you can never have too many mop buckets."

"Mop buckets?"

"That's right. You put each foot in a mop bucket

169

and grab hold of the handles. They'll work just like snowshoes. You'll walk over the snow. You'll be at the top of the hill before the police can crawl a yard and you can dance round the mayor like butterflies round a lamp post. A short, fat lamp post in Mayor Twistle's case."

"We'll need four mop buckets," Alice said.

"Not a problem . . . I collect them. After all, you can never have too many mop buckets."

Smiff went to the kitchen cupboard and pulled out four buckets. He and Alice slipped them on, grasped the handles and practised walking around the room.

It was clumsy but they soon got the idea.

Outside they could hear sharp raps of truncheons on doors as the constables climbed the hill and came ever closer.

"It's not over till it's over," Alice said. She opened the door and stepped out into the deep snow. Her mop bucket feet hardly sank through the surface of the snow and soon she was speeding up the hill. Smiff was close behind.

"Here! You two boys! Stop in the name of the law!" Constable Liddle shouted. "Stop or I'll call the police!"

He waved his rattle. He tried to move but every step was slow and clumsy. He gave up after five painful paces.

Mayor Twistle heard the rattles, and looked down the steep street. "We have them, James! Stop them!"

The mayor jumped down but the snow came above his knees. He was trapped like a wasp in honey.

Smiff and Alice strode past him. "Follow those thieves, James, and don't spare the horses!" the mayor roared but the driver was stuck in the snow as well. By the time they had climbed back on board the burglars had vanished.

Jack, the driver, struggled to turn the coach around. At last it was pointing south again. The two policemen came up to it, panting. "Mayor Twistle, sir, Mayor Twistle!" Liddle cried.

"We have your silverware, sir!"

The mayor's face turned bright as a gas lamp. "See! I knew I could defeat the villains of Wildpool! I knew it!"

And that was the way he told the tale.

TRIUMPH!

Mayor Twistle was delighted with the result, however. "I myself came face to face with the burglars. When they saw me they knew they had met their match. They dropped the loot and ran. They won't be doing any burgling for a long, long time. They know that they just can't get away with it. Not when I am in charge of Wildpool and have the backing of my magnificent police force!"

Mayor Twistle was asked if the burglars got away with anything valuable. He said that they stole a few of his wife's beads and a tin tea tray, but a rich man like him could afford it. One of his forks was bent and had some blood on the end but the mayor did not wish to say how it got there.

BE AWARE

House owners of Wildpool are warned to make sure they lock their doors at night and buy a guard dog as a pet. (Guard-cats and guard-goldfish are not so good.)

Of course you know that Mayor Twistle stretched the truth a bit. All right, he told a couple of whopping great lies. But Master Crook had been right. Give the victim back half of what you steal and they will think they have won. In fact that's just what Master Crook was about to tell his burglary students. . .

*

Samuel Dreep was waiting for Alice and Smiff as they clanked through the door of the Crime Academy.

They stepped out of their mop-bucket snowshoes and sank on to seats by the fire. Their clothes steamed in the heat.

Dreep's fingers fluttered in the firelight. "The school will be your home from now on," he said.

Alice shrugged. "I never had a home before so it makes no difference to me."

Dreep nodded. "And you, Smiff? You can't go home to live . . . not in that house now the police know about it."

Smiff sighed. "I can still see my mother, can't I?" Dreep nodded. "Then that's all right. Everyone has to leave home some time, don't they? And the beds here are better than at home anyway!"

That night the student burglars slept deep and dreamless sleeps. They were exhausted by their first day's work. The sun was over the horizon by the time they woke and already the melting snow was dripping from the roof.

Dreep served them breakfast of tea and toasted muffins then told them, "Master Crook will see you as soon as you've finished breakfast."

Alice and Smiff looked at one another. "I thought you said Dreep was Master Crook?" Smiff whispered.

"Yes. Well? So what? Have you never been wrong, monkey-face?" she replied.

They went to the basement door and walked down the steep wooden stairway to a stone-floored room in the cellar. It was lit by a single mutton-fat candle. There were chairs facing the far wall and a curtain hung over the door in that wall.

The curtain rippled as the door opened. But no one stepped through the curtain. Instead a soft, deep voice spoke through it.

"You did well, Alice and Smiff. If this school did exams then you would have passed your first one. Bert is safe and retired, and the jewels will sell for enough money to help the poor people of Wildpool."

"It was a close shave at times!" Alice argued.

"I know. We cannot have you doing that every night. The police will get to know the way you work and will catch you in the end. No, you will only be sent out when we need your special skills," the voice said.

"So what do we do?" Smiff asked. "Sit round here all day?"

"No," the dreamy voice said. "You will have lessons but you will learn new ways to separate the rich from their money and help the poor. There are more crimes than burglary, you know."

Alice was excited by the idea. "Who says? You says? Like what?" she asked.

"Ah! You will have to wait and see."

"What do you mean when you said we have to 'separate the rich from their money'?" Smiff asked. "You made us give half back to Mayor Twistle."

"Mmmm!" Master Crook agreed. "They make their money from their land, their mines, their factories and their shops. But it is the poor who sweat to do the work. It is the poor who end in the workhouse when they are too old or sick or weak to work any more. The rich won't pay to look after the poor . . . even though it's the poor who made their fortunes for them. So Master Crook's pupils will . . . help them to pay. We can't take away all of their money . . . but let's take some. It's a sort of tax."

"I'm all for that," Alice said.

"But it is a dangerous business," Master Crook said and the soft voice had a hard edge to it now. "If they

175

catch you their revenge will be terrible. I think we need a school trip to see the awful punishments they can give to the ones they catch! Perhaps we need a day in Darlham Gaol."

"School trip?" Smiff said. "Sounds interesting."

"Of course you will not spend all your time in the school," the voice said. "You, Alice, need to go back to your corner selling matches from time to time. I need you to report to me who is suffering there on the streets."

"Tell you who needs our help?" she said.

"Exactly. And you, Smiff, will go into the mines, the shipyards and the factories to see who is suffering there. You are my eyes and ears in Wildpool."

"I can do that!" Smiff said eagerly. "But . . . I mean . . . Alice and I can't save the world on our own . . . no matter what your teachers teach us. The world is just too wicked!"

Master Crook sighed. "I know. Other pupils will join you. Each will bring some new skill. In fact Mister Dreep tells me there is a new classmate waiting to meet you right now. Go and make her feel welcome."

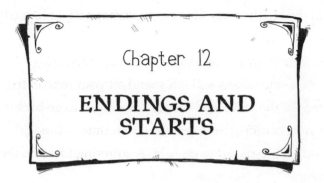

Chapter 12

ENDINGS AND STARTS

Constables Larch and Liddle stopped at the door to the police station before they went in. People were coming out on to the slushy streets to shop. The two constables bent their knees and spoke with one voice, as Inspector Beadle had taught them. "Mornin' all!"

They went inside and finished writing their report before they went home to sleep that morning.

Date:

5th. January 1837

The above burglary has been solved. The criminal,
Bert the Burglar, escaped justice but was driven
from Wildpool, never to return. We have started to
sweep the streets of Wildpool clean of the filth that
fouls its gutters (as the mayor puts it). The streets
of the town have now been cleaned of one burglar.
His young assistants will not be able to operate
without their leader. Plus a large quantity of silver was
rescued. All in all a great result for the Wildpool
police force.

PC Septimus Liddle (PC 01)
PC Archibald Larch (PC 02)

At 13 South Drive the fire was burning warm in the
living room. Mayor Twistle stood with his back to
the fire and polished his gold-rimmed spectacles on a
silken handkerchief. His back was hot. But the heat in

Arabella Twistle's brain burned hotter. "I have lost my jewels, Oswald, and you do not care."

The little man sighed. "Arabella, we took them from an old man in payment for a house we owned."

"It was a fair swap," the wide-chested woman stormed.

"It was a damp, worm-eaten cottage and the old man died within a year. When he died we took the cottage back. The jewels cost us nothing really," he smirked.

Lady Twistle leaned forward and prodded her husband with her fat finger. "I do not like to see crime go without punishment – crime and punishment go together like . . . like. . ."

"Like you and me, my sweet?"

"Like . . . birds of a feather. I want someone to pay for the theft of my jewels. I want someone to suffer."

"And so they shall, my dear. So they shall. I promise. In fact I made them suffer as soon as I got home last night. No one tangles with a Twistle and gets away with it."

Lady Twistle sat down quietly. "I am pleased to hear it, Ossie. Pleased."

The owner of Wildpool hardware shop was a happy man. He had checked his stock and found that someone had robbed him of a mop bucket that week. Maybe it had been that skinny boy with the ragged black hair, he thought.

Never mind. Sir Oswald Twistle's butler had just been into the shop to order a brand new, solid silver serving tray. That would make the shopkeeper, and the silver workers, enough money to get them through the winter. The thin old man, as grey as Smiff's blanket, turned a little bit pink with pleasure.

Alice and Smiff rose to their feet.

"Will we see you again?" Alice asked the curtain, then made a 'tut' sound. "Not that we're 'seeing' you now exactly!"

"When I need to tell you something . . . or sometimes when you need to tell me something," Master Crook said.

"And will we ever get to see your face? Find out who you are?"

"Better not," the voice said. "For you will see me

in the streets and theatres, taverns and town hall . . .
anywhere in Wildpool. It would not be good for us
to show that we recognize one another. Liddle and
Larch are not the cleverest law officers in the world.
But there are others who are more cunning and could
catch us out."

"Like their Inspector Beadle?" Alice asked.

"He's a sly one is Beadle," Master Crook said softly.
The curtain rippled and a door closed softly.

Alice walked towards it. "I want to see him. . ." she
said.

"Leave it," Smiff said. "We just have to trust him.
Sooner or later we have to trust someone." He looked
at her. "After last night I know I can trust you."

Alice scowled at him. "I should think so too. I
saved your life with my mop bucket idea!" Smiff's jaw
dropped with shock that she could say such a thing.

"Let's go and see our new classmate," he said and
led the way up the stairs to the classroom.

A girl in a poor black dress and shawl was turned
away from them, looking out of the window at the
gangs of men sweeping the snow from the streets so
the fine carriages could slosh through the slush. She

was about the same age as Smiff and Alice but her shoulders were broader. They seemed bent under the weight of a weary world.

She turned and her pale moon face smiled at the burglars, uncertain. "Hello again," she said.

"Nancy?" Alice gasped. "I thought you had a job as maid-servant to the Twistles."

Nancy nodded. "They threw me out when they lost the Twistle treasure. Lady Arabella said it was odd that someone picked the precious stuff and left the glass. She said it must have been someone who knew . . . someone like me."

"She couldn't prove anything," Smiff argued.

"She doesn't have to. She just sacked me – after she'd given me a beating. She wouldn't even give me a letter to get another job. I'd be on the streets without a penny . . . but Mr Dreep said he could help. He said I could learn a new trade here."

Dreep hurried into the room and rubbed his hands.

"So what trade are we going to learn?" Alice asked.

"We are going to learn highway robbery," Dreep said.

"That's an old one," Alice said.

"Ah, but we are going to invent a new way of using it. We are going to invent a completely new crime! When do you want to start?"

"As my old granny used to say, 'there's no time like the present'," Smiff grinned.

"Who says? You says?" Alice laughed. "I thought your granny said you can never have too many mop buckets?" she argued.

Smiff shrugged. "She said that too. You never can have too many mop buckets . . . and I think we found out why last night!"

Alice nodded. "Right! No time like the present. Let's get started!"

What a strange way to end a story, you cry. With a beginning. It isn't normal, I agree. But then, neither was Master Crook's Crime Academy.

THE END

LOOK OUT FOR MORE

MASTER CROOK'S
CRIME ACADEMY

ESCAPADES COMING SOON!

MASTER CROOK'S
CRIME ACADEMY

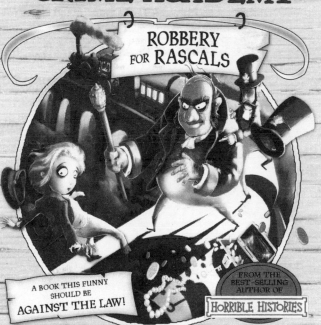

ROBBERY FOR RASCALS

A BOOK THIS FUNNY
SHOULD BE
AGAINST THE LAW!

FROM THE
BEST-SELLING
AUTHOR OF

HORRIBLE HISTORIES ™

TERRY DEARY

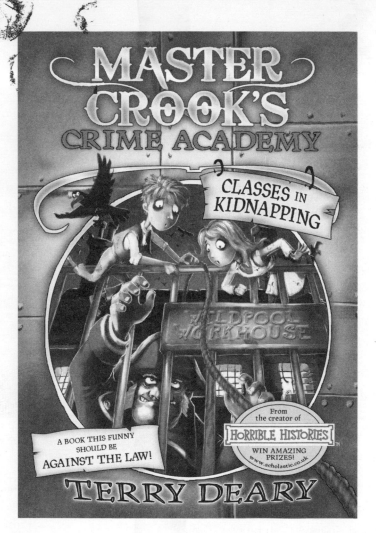

MASTER CROOK'S CRIME ACADEMY

CLASSES IN KIDNAPPING

WILDPOOL WORKHOUSE

A BOOK THIS FUNNY
SHOULD BE
AGAINST THE LAW!

From the creator of
HORRIBLE HISTORIES ™
WIN AMAZING PRIZES!
www.scholastic.co.uk

TERRY DEARY